I0627952

Grave Markers
Volume 4

Joseph Rubas, A.P. Sessler,

and Neil Davies

A
Grinning Skull Press
Publication

Bridgewater, MA 02324

The Skull logo with stylized lettering was created for Grinning Skull Press by Dan Moran, http://dan-moran-art.com/.
Cover designed by Jeffrey Kosh, http://jeffreykosh.wix.com/jeffreykoshgraphics.

ISBN: 1-947227-10-6
ISBN-13: 978-1-947227-10-1

CONTENTS

A WORD ABOUT GRAVE MARKERS

I promise to keep this short so you can get on to reading the tales collected in this volume. Folks often ask about Grave Markers and what they are. Grave Markers are, in a word, novelettes. They are stories too long to be included in anthologies (which usually average 5,000 to 7,000 words) but not quite long enough to be published on their own as stand-alone novellas. They are published individually in digital formats, and then later compiled into a print collection. The reason why we started this line is we often heard authors commenting that there wasn't a market for those "in-between" length stories and we wanted to give them an outlet for such pieces. And that about sums it up. Told you I'd keep it short. Now, without further ado, I present to you the premier collection of Grave Markers. Enjoy!

Michael J. Evans
Grinning Skull Press

GRAVE MARKER

Joseph Rubas

THE FREAKS
COME OUT
AT NIGHT

Prologue

The tall man whistled as he strolled along the rusted train tracks, the cheery tune echoing in the long, damp tunnel. A series of overhead lights lit his way, bathing the path with harsh pools of murky yellow, but he didn't need them; he could see perfectly in the dark. In fact, they stung his eyes, and with the wave of a hand, they went dark.

Overhead, a train rumbled past on its way to Brooklyn; the walls shook, and bits of debris fell from the ceiling. The man stopped, cocked his head, and listened as the roar reached its crescendo and then faded away. Despite the walls around him, he could smell the hot, tangy blood of the passengers, the dead-eyed morning commuters dragged from their beds and into the predawn world by materialistic need and crammed into rusted subway cars like sardines.

Money.

It was always money. Men killed themselves for money. They killed others. They killed things and places and hopes and dreams. They begged for money. Sold themselves for money. Stole money. Embezzled and extorted money. He grinned. He was beyond the need for money, beyond the need for anything.

Well, anything except blood.

Picking up his tune where he left off, the man started down the tracks once more. Seeing better in the dark than he had in the half-light, he noted the chips, cracks, and pockmarks marring the stone. Here was a piece of graffito: a giant phallus with the legend JUST DO IT scrawled below. There, on the other side and down a bit, was a Bible passage. He knew the verse well enough, for even demons quote scripture:

He will wipe away all tears from their eyes. There will be no more death, no more grief or crying or pain. The old things have disappeared.

— Revelation 21:4

His whistle slackened a bit as he passed it, eyeing the white, chalky scribble the way a nervous child would a cemetery or a dark stand of forest. A shiver went through him, and he picked up his pace.

"Of all the obscenities..." he muttered, his voice failing to echo in the chamber. He snickered. What a fine night it was. Five levels above him, Manhattan was starting to come alive, its streets filling with a flood of a thousand mortals. The lights along Broadway and in Times Square would start going dark soon as the sun rose over the East River, dappling its surface with vibrant gold, and day would reign. He tried to imagine the sight, but found that he couldn't. It had been so long since he looked upon the face of the sun. Six hundred years?

Seven? He was perturbed to find that he couldn't quite recall, but smiled again when he realized that it didn't matter. Time was a human construct. All the hours, minutes, and seconds of the day meant nothing to him, for he stood outside the normal flow of human life. To him, there was only day and night. During the former, he slept, and during the latter, he hunted.

And presently, deep below the bustling streets of New York City, the crossroads of the world, as some would call it, the man was hunting. Not the usual, hunter-gatherer hunt of his ancestors, stalking uncertainly through the shadows, with always the possibility of his prey escaping heavy upon his soul. No. He was hunting the way an old woman hunted for shortening in a supermarket, for in the network of tunnels, passages, and access corridors beneath the city, an entire legion of people lived and loved. They were dirty, penniless, and dressed only in rags. They were the fabled Mole People, eking out a miserable existence in a dark, subterranean hell little imagined by surface dwellers. In the 1970s and 1980s, they numbered in the tens of thousands, though beginning in 1989, agents of the city government had steadily whittled away the population through arrest, commitment, and deportation. As of 2011, there were less than ten thousand souls below the streets of New York, though Hurricane Sandy, which flooded the tunnels in 2012 had reduced them to, perhaps, half of that.

The man recalled all the fanciful tales he had heard. That the people lurking in the shadows here were blind and deaf, and they hunted human flesh (in the form of interlopers) by scent alone. In the glory days of the 70s, whispered rumors had police officers and city maintenance workers too scared to go into the tunnels. The tabloids reported a steady stream of missing people last seen descending into the hell below New York City. Firebrands on AM radio warned that one day the Mole People would rise up and take NYC from the surface people.

Rubbish. All of it.

At least until now.

Yes, the Mole People would rise up and take the city, but they wouldn't be people. They would be dead.

Dead, but still alive.

But that was in the future. For now, his only concern was locating the storied Mole People. He had been in the tunnels since dusk the previous evening, but had come across only one person, an elderly black man. Oh, they were here, like rats in the wall; one only had to find them.

Ahead, as if on cue, a tiny figure darted across the tracks and disappeared into one of the many fissures in the walls. He stopped, sniffed the air, and knew that it was a girl, roughly twelve or thirteen, barely out of childhood, but certainly no child; on the surface, children once married that young and bore children of their own. He remembered the primal forests of Europe in the lightless 17th century; villages, like tiny pinpricks of light, huddled against the darkness surrounding him. He encountered fifteen-year-old widows then, old women barely out of their twenties. Stupid. Dirty. Afraid. Cowering before the boot of a cruel god like a bunch of scolded bloodhounds.

Had this girl here, under the tracks, lived in 1748, she would be married now, perhaps to a rich landowner, but more likely to a lowly peasant.

"Little girl," the man said, his voice smooth and calming. "Little girl, I won't hurt you." He took a step forward and stuck out his hand, the way one would on meeting an anxious dog.

"Little girl, I want to help you ... I have candy."

It was working. The hypnotic sound of his voice was drawing her out. First, her head, sniffing the air like a ferret emerging from its burrow. Then her tiny body. She was wearing the tattered remains of a red hooded sweatshirt over rotting pink material that may have once been a dress. She stood close to her fissure, ready to climb back in if threatened, and watched with wide eyes. The man wasn't sure if she could see him or not. Her eyes must be *somewhat* adjusted to the dark.

Putting on a smile, the man took another step forward. "Come, my child. Come to me."

She started forward.

Closer.

The man smiled again. Genuinely, this time.

When she was close, he laid one hand on her head; her hair was tangled and matted. Under the rich smell of her blood, he could smell her fear, her dirtiness, her unwashed unmentionables.

He pushed down on her head, and she obediently dropped to her knees.

"Yes. Bow before your King."

He *was* the king now.

And soon, all the world would be his kingdom.

Chapter One

Detective Frank Burger, NYPD, pulled the Crown Vic to the curb before a crumbling tenement building and killed the engine. In the passenger seat, his partner, Martha Dessoye, unbuckled her seatbelt. "Hell of a day for a murder," she said, her brown eyes hard and guarded.

"It's *always* a hell of a day for murder," Frank replied, unfastening his own safety belt. Ahead, two blue-and-whites idled at the curb, one under a NO PARKING sign. Yellow crime scene tape fluttered in the frosty January breeze.

The four uniforms he could see were clustered around the vic. One of them was talking to a Middle Eastern man who kept pointing and making gestures with his hands. Frank could lip read fairly well and saw the man say: "…the subway…I don't know."

Glancing across the street, he saw a big double flight of stairs partially obscured by an aqua-green iron enclosure roughly waist high to a man. People went down and came up, but only a few: The major subway rush hours were early in the morning and late in the evening.

"What are you looking at?" Martha asked, craning her neck to see.

Frank nodded. "That guy said something about the subway."

"Like that's where the killer went?"

"I dunno. Let's find out."

They got out of the car, an Arctic wind slicing through them: Frank shuddered, but over the shiny roof of the unmarked car, Martha hadn't even flinched. Instead, she said flatly, "Remind me again why I'm not a cop in Miami."

"Because you look fat in pastels."

Martha cocked a dangerous look at him, and he couldn't help but laugh. "Watch it, smartass."

Just as they walked up, the Middle Eastern man held up a hand and ducked into a doorway. Frank looked at the faded wood sign posted above the entrance. DRY CLEANERS.

"That the owner?" Martha asked Sargent Jake O'Donnell.

"Yep," O'Donnell replied. Wearing a black windbreaker and a black cap, both emblazoned with the NYPD logo, O'Donnell was a big man. Six-foot-two, two-hundred pounds. He wore a thick brown mustache that made him look like he was in a Village People cover band and had dopey hazel eyes that belied the supercop within.

"I thought Asians had the corner on dry cleaners," Martha said, shaking her head. She was wearing a gray suit, the blazer of which was open to reveal the white shirt underneath—along with her gun and her badge.

"Near east, far east, what's the difference?"

Martha shrugged. "So what're we looking at?"

The body was under a white sheet held down with bricks to keep it from flying away in the breeze. Frank could see the sharp, pointed lines of a face underneath.

"Looks like a working girl," O'Donnell said. He lowered his epic bulk to his knees and pulled back the sheet. The woman was youngish, platinum blonde hair, pink lip gloss. She was almost as white as the sheet covering her.

"What makes you think she's a working girl?" Martha asked, putting her hands on her hips.

"Who else wears a two-foot-long roll of condoms in their fuck-me pumps?"

Martha shrugged, acquiescing.

"Cause of death?" Frank asked, looking pointedly away from the girl. He had been a homicide detective for eighteen years and had learned well enough to keep his emotions from getting in the way of his job, but looking into the face of a vic always caught him getting emotional.

"Her throat," O'Donnell said. When Frank looked at him quizzically, he added, "Someone ripped it out."

Frank couldn't stop a wince.

"Ripped it out?" Martha asked. "Like…with their teeth?"

O'Donnell nodded.

"Jesus," Martha breathed, looking at Frank.

"The owner here, Muhammad Atwarh, saw it happen. He's the one who called us."

As if on cue, Atwarh appeared from the doorway of his shop. "I had to take that call," he said in clear, but heavily-accented English.

"You saw it go down?" Martha asked instantly.

Atwarh nodded. "I saw the whole thing."

"Invite us inside and let's talk about it," she said.

Inside, Atwarh's shop was a typical dry cleaners, save for the Islamic style portraits and trinkets on the wall. In his tiny office, Atwarh sat in a creaky, old kitchen chair.

"Tell us what happened," Frank said.

Atwarh nodded. "I was opening up my shop when I heard the woman scream."

"What time?" Martha interjected. She was holding a pen and a pad of paper.

Atwarh considered. "Six, I think. It was still dark outside."

Martha nodded. "Then what?"

"Well, I went outside, and I saw him attacking her. He had her head pushed to one side like he was kissing her neck." He demonstrated with his hands, pushing an imaginary head against an imaginary shoulder and going in for an imaginary smooch. "I said 'Hey!' and he saw me and ran away."

"Where did he go?" Frank asked, though he suspected he already knew the answer.

"He went into the subway," Atwarh said, gesturing and then dropping his hands to his lap in frustration.

"What did he look like?" Martha asked.

"He looked," Atwarh said seriously, "like a *djinni*."

"A what?" Frank asked.

"A demon from Arabic folklore," Martha said without looking up.

Atwarh smiled and pointed to Martha as though she truly under-stood him. "Yes. A *djinni*. He had black eyes and a white face. When he saw me, he dropped the girl and hissed like a cat." He shuddered.

"Was he tall?" Frank asked. "Short? Fat?"

"He was tall and skinny. Like a corpse. And he had no hair on the top of his head. He was bald. I think he was a white man, but he was so pale he could have been anything."

"Except black," Frank said.

"Nope," Martha said, shaking her head. "I've seen black people get really pale."

Atwarh nodded. "When I fought in the war, I had a black friend. A bomb blew his legs off, and he got so white he looked like milk."

"What war did you fight in?" Martha asked, snapping closed her notepad to indicate the question was social rather than business.

"Desert Storm," Atwarh said instantly. "I fought for my country … America."

"Thank you for your service," Martha said, nodding.

Atwarh nodded his appreciation. "I have not seen my family in Iraq for almost thirty years. They disowned me. But I did what was right."

As they were leaving, Atwarh called to them. "Tell me when you find him. I would like to do right with him." Grinning maliciously, he throttled an imaginary neck.

Outside, in the cold, Martha shook her head. "Guess we got a de-mon on our hands."

"Better call up the *Ghostbusters*," Frank said, sliding a pair of sunglasses from his breast pocket.

"You thinking what I'm thinking?"

"That he saw a junkie?"

Martha nodded. "That's what I'm thinking."

An hour later, they had the surveillance tapes from the camera overlooking the stairs into the subway, and also from the cameras monitoring the platform. If a skinny bald guy ran down those stairs at six in the morning, they'd know by lunch time, and given the sophisticated nature of modern recording equipment, they'd very likely have his face on the evening news come six 'o'clock.

Chapter Two

Beast House; Malcasa Point, CA: Built in grand Victorian style during 1902, the Beast House today remains one of the most fascinating "haunted houses" in America. Over the span of nearly a hundred years, over a dozen people have died violently in its walls. That they have died is irrefutable fact, not lore. The most recent death attributed to the Beast House occurred in December 2015, when Danny "The Gypsy" Parsons, host of a popular AM radio show dedicated to the paranormal, was killed during an unsanctioned midnight visit. On December 15, Parsons jimmied open a back door, determined to spend the night, and within an hour, after failing to respond to text messages from his producer who was waiting in a van parked nearby, he was found dead, his stomach having been ripped open by something with powerful claws. His passing was reported in many respectable publications, including the New York Times, The Richmond Democrat, and...

Harvey Goldblum stopped typing and sat back in his leather office chair, a burning disquiet bubbling in his stomach. He read over what he had written, deemed it garbage, and with a click of a button, it was gone. The Word document before him was crisp and white, like freshly fallen snow, the cursor blinking insistently, seeming to urge him to hurry up and get started RIGHT NOW. In his present mood, he wanted to reach through the screen, grab it, and throttle it until it died. It was almost as bad as that paperclip carton Word used years ago. What was his name? Clippy? Snippy? Harvey couldn't remember, but clearly recalled his frustration when it would pop up in the middle of his writing. "It looks like you're writing a letter," it would say, obscenely winking one of its googly eyes, the text appearing in a comic strip-like speech bubble. "Let's get started."

Though he supposed he should have appreciated the offer of assistance, Harvey Goldblum knew damn well how to write a letter. He didn't need some pushy cartoon character to pop up from nowhere and hijack his computer screen.

If it could help me get my mojo back, Harvey thought, watching the cursor flash, *then I might be interested.*

Harvey sighed. It had been…what, ten years since he last wrote something? Before the accident and the long, subsequent dry spell; before the sleepless nights and the uncomfortable mental constipation; before the fidgety feeling and his terror of the computer. There was a time not so long ago that he couldn't even bring himself to sit down in front of the thing. Just thinking about it gave him the shakes.

Gradually, he stopped breaking out into hives at the mere mention of the word "computer," and before long he got restless, the way he used to when he wasn't writing. He would pace the floors, his hands clasped behind his back, and find himself thinking of how he would word things. A mailman would come to the door and, after thanking him and sending him on his way, he would mentally recreate their encounter, detailing everything from the way his lank hair rustled in the breeze to the sickly coughing noise his truck made as he pulled out of the driveway. What could he say? He was a writer. He couldn't help it.

Pursing his lips, Harvey started typing again:

Rising along the eastern flank of US20...

No. He didn't like it. He hit the backspace button until the document was clean once more.

Maybe I've lost it, he thought, a sudden chill spreading through his soul. *Maybe I'll never write again.*

Harvey was surprised at the sense of loss he felt. He had been writing since he was thirteen, when he would sit with a pen and a pad of paper under a tall oak tree in his parents' backyard, drawing inspiration from the way the sunlight filtered through the branches and danced on the paper. His earliest efforts were space operas in the style of Bradbury and Clarke. As his interest in the paranormal blossomed, however, and he began visiting occult bookstores in Boston and New York City, he found himself called (and that's exactly how he felt— "called") to chronicle real-life terrors, tales of haunted houses, UFOs, Mothmen, and astral projection. His first nonfiction book, *Myths of New England*, was released in 1985 through a small publishing company in Springfield Mass. Though it sold poorly, he remembered even now the heady rush of accomplishment he felt holding it in his hands. Over thirty years later, flipping through the pages of his own book remained his happiest memory.

To think that it was all over …

Sighing, Harvey pushed away from the desk and got up. Padding through the living room, all hardwood floors and white furniture, he pulled his silken robe closed with a swish, relishing the feel of it against his naked skin. In the kitchen, he took a bottle of wine from a high cabinet and, grabbing a long-stem glass, poured a measure out for himself. Leaning against the counter and gazing out the bay windows overlooking the Long Island Sound, he sipped his wine and thought about what he would do with his time if he could no longer write. Paint? He wasn't much of an artist. Garden? Gag me with a spoon, as they used to say. There *were* the consulting jobs that came in every once in a while: Whenever the Travel Channel wanted to do a piece on ghosts or ghouls, he *could* agree to serve as an "expert"; sit in front of a camera and talk. Hollywood, too, came to him from time to time.

Yeah. Sure. Great.

But that's not what he wanted to do.

He wanted to *write*.

He wanted to cry, scream, stomp his feet, and smash the wine glass against the wall *because he couldn't write.*

Chapter Three

"Vic's name is Valerie Baldwin," Martha said, slapping a file on the desk. Frank, hitherto watching the surveillance video on the computer, picked it up and opened it.

The first thing he saw was the mugshot. Valerie Baldwin, blonde and haggard, looked strung out, dark circles under her pale hazel eyes. He took the picture out and sat it on the keyboard. Next were the papers detailing her criminal history, several priors dating back to 2011, mainly for prostitution and drug possession, though there was a criminal trespass thrown in for variety.

Frank grabbed the glossy mugshot and looked at it once more before putting it back in the folder. She was a pretty girl. Looking into her eyes, he couldn't help but wonder how she came to where she was then, using and selling herself on the corner of 34th Street. Many hookers have genuine sob stories. Abuse. Neglect. Poverty. What was Valerie's? And...what could she have been if things had gone right for her?

Sighing, he handed the folder back to Martha. "What do the

tapes show?" she asked, sitting. The bullpen was a flurry of activity: Phones ringing, people talking. He could barely hear her over the din.

"Not a damn thing," he said, turning back to the screen. The subway platform was rendered in grainy, soundless black and white. The timestamp said 6:08 a.m. The platform was crowded, so it was possible he just wasn't seeing the perp, but the video from the stairs didn't show him either. "No skinny bald guys."

"You think Atwarh's lying?" Martha asked, leaning closer to the screen. Frank caught a whiff of her perfume. Though she didn't use a lot, the scent assaulted his nose.

"Maybe," Frank said. "It's possible. Do we have anything on Baldwin? Friends? Family?"

Martha shook her head. "Not on file. Her pimp was Tyrone Steele, but he's in prison."

Frank recognized the name. Only later did he remember that Steele, AKA Black Angus, shot two NYPD officers during a routine traffic stop in 2012.

Looking at the crush of humanity jostling on the platform, Frank sighed. So far they had a murder victim, one (possibly unreliable) witness, and nothing else. Frank couldn't count the number of cold cases he'd dealt with over the years that began with similar circumstances. The murder rate in New York was at an all-time low, but a small percentage of those murders went unsolved. And then you had the murders of the past. Frank didn't know the number off hand, but he believed that there were at least 10,000 cold case killings on the books. Too damn many.

And it looked like Valerire Baldwin might become one of them.

"Our best shot is the bite mark on her neck," Frank said thoughtfully, watching as a train slid into the station onscreen. Before turning Baldwin over to the medical examiner, they took a plaster cast of the teeth marks. With any luck, they'd be able to get a good likeness. If the bastard's teeth weren't on file, they could take it around to all the dentists in the city. Frank knew that that wasn't much, but it was something.

"I wanna bring Atwarh in," Martha said. "Have him talk to a sketch artist. See if maybe we can crack him...*if* he's hiding something."

Frank thought of the little Iraqi. He doubted Atwarh committed the killing. *Who murders someone and then calls the cops on themselves? To be fair, though, he could have thought that by placing the call, he'd be least suspected. Crafty.*

"CSI pick anything up?"

Martha shrugged. "I haven't heard back from them yet. You'd think they'd get *something.*"

"It won't be a hair," Frank said, "if we're looking for a bald guy."

"Probably skin under her nails."

Frank nodded, looked away from the screen. His eyes felt grainy and his neck was beginning to ache. He checked his watch and found that he had been sitting in front of the computer for nearly three hours. He was suddenly aware of his rumbling stomach and his dry, tacky throat.

"You okay?" Martha asked, genuine concern in her voice.

"Yeah, I'm fine," he said, waving a hand. "I just need a break."

As if on cue, Captain Leary poked his head out from his office.

"Can I see you two, please?"

"Saved by the bell," Martha said, standing.

Leary, a tall, broad spruce of a man with a neat crew cut and a mustache, dominated the shadowy corner office. Sitting before the massive oak desk, Frank couldn't help but gaze at the framed photos, degrees, commendations, certificates, and letters decorating the dark blue walls, even though he knew their contents and nature just as well as Leary, if not better. There, by the filing cabinet, was a letter from George W. Bush dated September 15, 2001, thanking Leary for his service during the 9/11 attacks (Leary, a detective at the time, rushed into the North Tower and managed to drag a dozen people from the building before it collapsed). And there, sitting on Leary's desk, but facing his guests like a trophy, was a picture of him with Barack Obama taken at a White House dinner in 2010.

"What do you got?" Leary asked. There was only one thing he could be referring to.

"Not much," Frank admitted, squirming in his seat like a man in a Preparation H commercial. "We're bringing in our only witness later to talk to Peterson." Peterson was the sketch artist. "We also took a cast of the bite mark on her neck. When forensics is done, we're hoping to have something we can shop around to local dentists."

Leary nodded curtly. "You say you think it was a junkie?" He asked the question of Martha, not Frank.

"Possibly, sir," she said. "We're hoping to find a likely candidate in the database. If we can find a big bald guy with prior convictions for drugs, we might find our man."

"Alright," Leary said by way of dismissal. "Keep me posted."

Back in the bullpen, Frank eased into his chair. "You hungry?" Martha asked.

"Yeah."

"Wanna go somewhere?"

Frank glanced at the computer. "No. Just order in, I guess."

"The usual?"

Forty-five minutes later, Martha met the pizza boy in the lobby, and she and Frank ate at their joint desk, Frank barely tasting his food. He rewound the surveillance video time and time again, but never saw a big bald man.

Something wasn't right.

If the perp ran down those stairs, the camera would have given them a clear view of his face.

Later, when Atwarh came in, they questioned him for nearly an hour. After he left, Frank said to Martha, "His story didn't change."

They tried every deceitful tactic in the book to get Atwarh to slip up, but he stuck to his story, and, Frank thought, his eyes shone with honesty.

"No, it didn't."

He gave Peterson a description. When the sketch artist was done, Frank held the picture in his hands for a long time, looking at it. The man's face was drawn, his eyes dark and his teeth bared. He looked like a demon.

Just like Atwarh said.

At least we have something, Frank thought.

Chapter Four

The man walked slowly along Broadway, under the gaily lit marquees, breathing richly of the cold city air. People passed him in droves even though it was close to eleven on a Tuesday night, and as they did, he savored the coppery scent of their blood.

For him, the night began early; he rose before sunset and walked the caves crisscrossing the metro area, hunting for any stragglers who had somehow managed to elude him and his people. The only one he found was an old woman crammed into a cardboard box near a ladder leading up to the level above. She was crazy, he saw in an instant, and when she wouldn't heed his siren's call (the mentally impaired are naturally resistant to hypnotism; he didn't know why), he dragged her out by her throat and sank his teeth into her warm, pulsing jugular.

Not too long after his meal, the others began to stir, and by eight o'clock, the tunnels were jammed with a shambling mass of living dead. Wanting to be alone, he crawled to the first level, the active subway tunnel, and then through a manhole in an alley between two crumbling buildings. A black man hiding amongst the rubbish and refuse saw him and, grinning, pulled a knife from his jacket pocket.

"Mister Sewer Man," he said, advancing. "What you got for me?"

Having just eaten, Mr. Sewer Man simply snapped the miscreant's neck, holding him close as he went limp, as though he could absorb some of the thug's departing vitality.

Now, whistling lightly, the man rounded a bend and before him, as bright as the summer sun, Times Square unfurled, its many banners, tickers, and video screens assailing the eyes, demanding attention *now*. Cars, mainly taxis, moved slowly along the streets and avenues, honking, stopping, starting, honking again.

People rushed back and forth, streaming from one side of the broad avenue to the other. Many of them were young. Hipsters or trust funders with nothing to rise early for. Their blood was the sweetest. The man moved slowly through the crowd flooding the sidewalk, doing a little dance as he went. *Soon*, he thought, facing the black sky, *soon this would all belong to me.*

Mr. Sewer Man.

Chapter Five

It's too early for this, Frank Burger thought as Martha parked the Crown Vic next to a NO PARKING sign and killed the engine. *Way too early.*

It was 7:03 a.m. to be exact; the sun, dazzling but heatless, had only just crested over the city, its rays creeping along the streets like questing fingers. Here, on the edge of Hell's Kitchen, tall brownstones blocked most of the sunlight, leaving West 39th Street in shadows.

After visiting the coroner at eight the previous evening (Frank hated the tiny tiled room where the bodies were kept, the chill permeating the air, the stench of disinfectant), he and Martha parted ways, Frank returning to his little apartment overlooking West 81st Street. He ate a frozen pizza and was in bed by ten.

At six thirty, the phone rang. It was Martha, already on the job. "Get dressed. We got another stiff."

"Another?" Frank asked, his heart dropping. "As in, another stiff whose neck was eaten?"

"Of course that's what I meant. Get dressed. I'll be there in ten."

And thus began another day as a New York City homicide detective.

"Come on, lazy," Martha said, slapping him on the knee; he jerked, and only then did he realize he had been daydreaming.

Outside, a frigid wind washed over them, and for a minute Frank had a sense of déjà vu so strong it scared him: yellow police tape dancing in the breeze; uniforms talking to people clustered on a street corner; a body under a sheet. The real difference here, Frank saw, was that today's vic was lying not on the sidewalk, but in the middle of the street, a red Ford Focus standing nearby, the driver's side door standing open. People lined the sidewalk on the far side of the street, some pointing, some holding their hands to their mouths in shock, and some, Frank saw with a flash of anger, recording the whole thing on their cellphones, probably so they could post it to Youtube later. He wanted to yell, to scream (*Someone's dead! Have a little respect!*), but Martha, seeing his jaw clenching, put her hand on his arm. "You alright?" she asked, her normally hard-edged voice (*My bitch tone*, she called it) replaced by soft concern.

"I'm fine," he said.

Sargent O'Donnell was talking to one of his men when they walked up. Sending him away, he looked at them, his hands unconsciously going to his generous hips. "We gotta stop meeting like this," he said.

"What happened anyway?" Martha asked.

O'Donnell told them: At 6:29 a.m., the vic—a black male, late twenties to early thirties, thin—was pulled from his car by three men and attacked in front of over a dozen witnesses. Several people tried to intervene, but wound up lying on the pavement.

"It's the same thing as yesterday," O'Donnell said. "Chewed his neck all to shit."

Frank and Martha glanced at each other. "Any of them a big bald guy?" Frank asked.

O'Donnell shook his head. "Nope."

Frank blinked. "No?"

"Looks like a different thing entirely," the sergeant said. "Same deal, different perps."

"Where are our witnesses?" Martha asked.

"Over there," O'Donnell said, nodding to a cluster of people standing just inside the tape. "We got their names, numbers, and addresses. Figured you'd want to talk to them at the station. "

Frank nodded.

"One of 'em got it on their phone. The attack, I mean."

Martha and Frank both jumped. "Video?" Frank asked.

O'Donnell nodded.

Suddenly Frank wanted to be back at the station, where they could talk to the witnesses and watch the video.

Then his spirits, high only a moment before, came crashing down. Two different murders committed separately, by different perps, and in both cases, the vic's neck was eaten. It may look like a coincidence on the surface, but Frank knew there was a link, and that meant four psychos were loose in the city, thirsty for blood.

It was going to be a long day.

Chapter Six

Harvey Goldblum rose each morning before dawn and jogged three miles from his spacious estate on Route 25, through a stand of forest, and around a lazy pond where geese wheeled and bathed, and back again. He wasn't a fitness nut by any means, but his physical therapist told him jogging at a steady pace would do wonders for his knee, and by the time he no longer *needed* to do it, he was so used to doing it that he never stopped.

Jogging? he remembered asking. It was November 2007. He had been out of the hospital for nearly three months, and just moving his left leg left him sweating and on the verge of passing out.

That's right, Kelly Johnson said. She was a fit woman with short blonde hair and small breasts. Harvey envied her beauty, but hated the bitch because she made him hurt himself day after day. *You'll have to work your way up to it, but once you get there, jogging is great.*

Harvey didn't know. Simply *existing* was a challenge.

It all began on the afternoon of June 28th. He was lost in thought, as always, and stepped onto a busy street in Brooklyn. He couldn't remember exactly what he had been thinking of, but it most likely had to do with writing. Whatever it was, it changed him: A car struck him at twenty miles per hour, throwing him ten feet through the air and onto the hard, unforgiving concrete below. He couldn't recall the accident itself, but could *clearly* remember being rushed into the emergency room, doctors and nurses running alongside him, shouting for this, yelling for that. *It was just like an episode of* ER, he thought dazedly, and passed out again. When he woke, the doctors told him they had thought he was going to die.

But he didn't.

I'm one tough mama jama, he remembered saying. When he was sixteen, his father threw him out of the house, saying he'd rather have no son at all than a queer, and for a time, he lived in a tent by a river. There was even a period where he pimped himself out to the middle-class closet queens infesting suburban Hartford, but he rarely ever thought of *that,* and certainly never *spoke* of it.

If I could survive that, he thought, *I can survive anything.*

Returning home, his body quivering pleasantly, a thin sheen of sweat slathering his skin, he checked the mailbox, out of habit than anything else—that lazy bitch of a mailman *never* came before noon, then grabbed the newspaper he'd neglected to get when he left. Sitting in the sun-washed breakfast nook and sipping at a cup of coffee, he scanned the headlines, lingering over one:

WOMAN MURDERED IN MANHATTAN.

The brief story detailed the killing of an unnamed hooker. Her throat had been ripped out, the article said, and Harvey shuddered at the thought. *What is this world coming to?*

Ruin. That's what.

Thinking of vampires, he went off to try to write.

Chapter Seven

"I don't get it," Frank said three hours later. He was sitting at the cold metal table dominating Interrogation Room #5, a sheaf of papers arrayed in front of him. Martha was leaning cross-armed against the one-sided mirror through which Captain Leary had watched as they talked to the eight witnesses who watched Donald Atkins, a twenty-eight-year-old Verizon store manager, get dragged from his car and cannibalized.

"He stopped," one of them, a woman named Maria, said, referring to Atkins. "And these three guys just came out of nowhere. They ripped open his door and pulled him out."

Maria said the three men ran east along West 48th Street. On a hunch, Frank pulled up Google Maps and found a subway station just around the corner.

There was the connection. These assholes were definitely linked to the guy who killed Valerie Baldwin.

But how?

Martha had suggested a cult. People still lived under the city, in the abandoned tunnels below the subway tracks; maybe some of them were coming up to the surface with a grudge. It made sense. At least as much sense as you could hope for.

"It's bigger than just Baldwin," Martha said now, nodding. "Too bad the video glitched."

"Yeah," Frank said. They found the cellphone footage to be unusable when they went to watch it. Through some technological fluke, everything was rendered in crystal-clear high def—except the perps.

They were invisible. Watching the video, it looked like Atkins was beset by ghosts instead of cannibals.

"I don't know about you," Martha was saying now. "But I'm starved. Lunch?"

Frank sighed, scanned the papers before him. Names. Numbers. Official statements. His vision blurred.

"Yeah."

When they got back, they would have to talk to Leary. By the end of the day, there would probably be a task force in place. So much work. So much activity. Frank needed some grub before he could face that.

Stretching, he got up, his back popping. "Ah, the joys of forty-five," he grunted as he tried to twist the stiffness out of his back.

From the interrogation rooms via the bullpen, they walked down a long hall flanked by doors and windows, then down a flight of stairs to the underground parking garage. Still sore, Frank moved stiffly, wincing as long tendrils of pain snaked into his shoulders.

"You look like Frankenstein," Martha chuckled.

"I *feel* like Frankenstein."

In the parking garage, the sounds of the city were distorted, like sounds heard underwater. "You ever see *The Walking Dead?*"

Frank shook his head. "No. Heard about it, though."

They were at the Crown Vic now, Martha climbing into the driver's seat. They took turns at the wheel, just as they took turns heading a crime scene. It was something they did. Equal division of work.

"You should check it out some time," she said, spinning the wheel and bringing the car onto 3rd Avenue. "It's really interesting."

"I heard it was bloody." Frank didn't like bloody movies or TV shows. He got enough of that crap during the day.

"Yeah, kinda," Martha replied, "but it's a good...social study, you know? Seeing how people react in the apocalypse."

The 17th Precinct was a tall metal-and-glass goliath on East 51st Street, a narrow lane winding through a forest of brick and mortar. Martha turned north and followed East 51st to Lexington Ave. After a crush of people hurried through the crosswalk, she turned right and drove a block to the intersection of East 53rd. To the left, a CVS pharmacy occupied a corner storefront. On their right, a parking lot fronted a small structure set apart from the other buildings. A sign over the door said DELI. The locals knew it as DELL'S because the owner's name was Jim Dellson. Because it was so close to the station house, a lot of cops grabbed lunch there. It helped that the food was good.

Lamenting the lack of good parking in the city, Martha pulled into a slot next to a white Prius and an Altima with a COEXIST bumper sticker.

"Who's paying?" Frank asked as he got out. A bitterly cold wind swept through the rising canyons around them. Though Frank had spent his entire life in New York City, he always felt a grip of claustrophobia in Mid-Town.

"I paid last time," Martha said, slamming the door.

Inside, the deli, arranged more like a diner, was packed. All the booths along the windows, all the stools at the counter. The sound of many voices speaking at once created a drab cacophony, broken only by the occasional peal of laughter and the scraping of forks against plates.

Frank shook his head. "Let's go somewhere else."

"You kidding?" Martha asked. "By the time we get somewhere else, it'll be time to head back. Did you see that traffic?"

"I saw a typical day in Manhattan," he said, giving up and letting Martha have her way.

"I saw your mother," Martha shot back.

Five minutes later, a booth at the north end of the restaurant cleared out, and after a busboy wiped it down and removed the cups, a waitress in a black T-shirt sat them.

"What can I get you to drink?" she asked, a pad of paper in her hand.

"Coffee," Martha said. And then, looking at Frank, "What do you want, cupcake?"

Frank's laugh surprised him. It was deep. Genuine. "Coffee, too," he said.

With a nod, the waitress took off.

"Cupcake, huh?"

She shrugged. "You look like a cupcake."

"That mean you wanna eat me?"

"I'm more of ribs and Jack Daniels kind of girl."

Their booth overlooked the intersection of Lexington and East 53rd. Cars crept by in the streets; people rushed along the sidewalks, some of them talking into their cellphones.

"I can see you chewing on a rib," Frank said.

Martha nodded. "I don't count calories."

"Why should you?"

"Because I look fat in pastels?"

Frank grinned. "Hey, I'm honest. Sue me."

The waitress returned with their coffee. "I'm sorry I can't give you guys a menu, but they'll all being used."

"Busy day, huh?" Martha asked.

She nodded. "Very busy."

"That's okay. We know what we want anyway, don't we, sweet-heart?"

"Two burgers, two fries."

The waitress jotted that down, mumbling soundlessly as she went. When she was done, she nodded and went away.

"You keep calling me silly names in public, I'm gonna have to re-port you to Internal Affairs."

"On what grounds?"

"Sexual harassment."

Martha let out a sharp, braying laugh. "Don't flatter yourself, honey. You ain't much to look at."

They lapsed into silence then, Martha playing on her smartphone and Frank watching the foot traffic on the sidewalk.

Martha chuckled.

"What?"

Frank glanced away from the window.

She chuckled again and shook her head. "Someone on my Facebook posted this picture of a big black dog and asked 'What would you name it?'"

"Yeah?"

"I said Michael Clarke Duncan."

Frank laughed. "You're a racist."

She replied, but Frank didn't hear her; something had caught his eye. Across the street, a bald black man in a black windbreaker ducked into the CVS after looking nervously around. There was something in his hand. It looked like a gun.

Frank swallowed.

The CVS doorway was dark from that angle. He couldn't see past the threshold, but he *did* see a woman running out, looking afraid.

"I think someone's robbing the CVS," Frank said.

"What?" Martha whipped around.

People were looking as the woman ran past. She started toward the deli.

"Come on!" Frank said, getting up.

He pushed past the people milling at the door, adrenaline beginning to course through his body. "Move," Martha shouted.

Outside, they met the woman in the middle of the parking lot. "He's got a gun!"

"Go inside!" Frank said, gesturing toward DELL's.

Martha had her radio in her hand. "1030 in progress. CVS, corner of Lexington and East 53rd."

Frank drew his gun as he crossed the street, suddenly oblivious to everything around him but the doorway ahead.

Despite what programs like *Law & Order* showed, detectives rarely engage in gunplay. Frank honestly couldn't remember the last time he and a perp were shooting at one another, couldn't honestly remember the last time he actually *handled* a perp. Blood pounded in his temples and his mouth went dry.

It had been a while.

What if something went wrong?

At the doorway, Frank flanked the left side while Martha took the right. She was holding her gun. Her eyes were wide and bright. Frank knew this is what she lived for. They had been partners going on six years; how many times had she lamented the lack of action?

"I'm going in," she said.

Frank shook his head. "It's too dangerous."

"I'm going in," she said.

Frank glanced back at DELL'S, as though expecting a second robber to be creeping up on them. When he looked back, Martha nodded and ducked through the door.

"Damn it," Frank hissed, and followed her.

What happened next went down so quickly that even later Frank had trouble putting it together. Martha was standing by a newspaper dispenser, her gun raised. She yelled, "Drop the weapon!"

Frank darted behind her, bumped into a cosmetic display, and brought his own weapon up.

The man was standing by the counter. Before Frank knew what was happening, the man was shooting and Martha was falling. Frank squeezed two shots off, both of which hit the gunman, knocking him against the counter, the gun flying from his hand.

Martha.

As two uniforms rushed through the door like the cavalry in the old movies, a day late and a dollar short, Frank dropped to his knees next to Martha. He was numb, didn't feel the warm blood seeping through the fabric of his pants.

Lucky shot, he thought later, dazed, like a bomb-blasted refugee. *He couldn't have aimed. He didn't have time.*

The shot, fired at random, could have gone anywhere. Past Martha. Into her vest. Into her shoulder. Into her guts even.

Instead, it went into her head.

Chapter Eight

Mr. Sewer Man emerged from the East 3rd Street subway station and stepped into the frosty night. Streetlamps cast pools of harsh orange light onto the sidewalks, and the row houses lining the narrow street were dark, their stoops, host to many drinking contests and bull sessions during the summer, stood empty, windswept, as though forlorn.

A few people hurried by him, oblivious, like all New Yorkers, to their surroundings. They didn't see him, didn't see the three ghouls behind him, their pale faces dirty and streaked with the dust so ubiquitous in the caverns below the subway. One of them, a woman wearing the tattered remains of a wool dress, hissed softly in the back of her throat, and he hushed her. "Not here," he whispered. They were too exposed. They would have to spread out into the streets and alleyways surrounding the stairwell. He sniffed the air and detected on it the scent of a thousand unseen meals, some asleep in the tenements across the way, others moving in the shadows. The pimps, pushers, junkies, and prostitutes. Scum of the city.

Mr. Sewer Man breathed deeply, sucking the smell of them into his lungs and then pushing it out again, savoring it the way a man would a glass of wine.

Across Manhattan Island, he knew, there were a dozen teams just like his own, four or five vampires crawling from gutters and man-holes, subways and basements, moving stealthily through the darkness, cast in the rising shadows of the Empire State Building, the Brooklyn Bridge, the One World Trade Center.

So, he thought, *it's finally come.*

"Come," he said to his flock, and started across the street. The sidewalk was dotted with barren trees, dead in the January cold. He moved among them, avoiding streetlights where he could. At an inter-section, the world dark and slumbering around them, he said, "Go."

And they did, moving in different directions, melding with the night. Soon, the city would be his.

Chapter Nine

Frank Berger twisted open a fresh bottle of Canadian Mist whiskey and poured himself a healthy shot, finishing it off with a splash of Coke. He took the drink into the living room and sat on the red loveseat his ex-wife, Maggie, left when she fled to Maine with the next door neighbor. Thinking of it soured Frank's already dark mood, and he took a drink, grimacing as the whiskey slid down his throat like lava.

It had only been a few hours since Martha Dessoye was killed in the middle of a CVS on Lexington Avenue, even less since Captain Steven Leary placed him on paid leave, but that time seemed eternal to him now. He glanced around the small apartment, from the tiny kitchen to the window overlooking West 81st Street, a narrow lane lined with brownstones and trees. He couldn't remember the last time he was sober.

Sighing, he sat the glass on the end table and picked up the remote. There was nothing good on. He liked *Impractical Jokers* on TruTV, but Martha was the one who turned him onto it, and seeing it reminded him of her, so he switched to Food Network, where Guy Fierri, in all his frosted-tipped splendor, was eating a cheeseburger and declaring it, "Out of bounds!"

I could have stopped her.

The thought came suddenly and unbidden, and for a moment, Frank wasn't entirely sure it hadn't been spoken aloud by some unseen force.

He sighed.

It was true.

He could have stopped her.

He *should* have stopped her.

He finished his whiskey and went to make himself another one. On the TV, Guy was driving into the sunset, talking to the camera from the driver's seat of a Camaro, or maybe it was a Mustang. Frank didn't know. Martha was dead, and he didn't know.

For the hundredth time he caught himself shaking his head. *She can't be gone. We were laughing and joking at lunch just a few hours ago.*

She was definitely gone. Died in the ambulance on the way to the hospital, Frank holding her hand and weeping unashamedly as the white-faced medic worked over her, eventually dropping back and shaking his head. *Sorry*, that gesture said. *There's nothing we can do. She's beyond us now.*

Six years he'd known her. Six. That was like twenty in cop years. There was no way she wouldn't be at the station waiting for him when he came back. No way in hell.

When he returned to the couch, he was surprised to find that he was crying again.

When the storm passed—One hour? Two?—he changed the channel and found himself staring at the morning news. Two anchors were sitting at a desk. What time was it? He checked his watch, realized he didn't have it on—Why would he? Time had no meaning —and went into the kitchen to look at the clock on the microwave. It said 6:10 in soft green.

"...witnesses say they fled into the subway."

Frank froze.

Subway?

Back in the living room, he stood drunkenly before the TV. On the screen, cops with assault rifles ran through predawn streets, waving people back. Another scene showed an ambulance screaming past, its lights and sirens blazing. It looked like something big happened. A ter-rorist attack maybe.

Frank sat heavily on the sofa and watched as the scene jumped back to the anchors behind their desk. By 6:45, he had the whole story: Several dozen people came from out of the shadows last night and attacked unaware New Yorkers before disappearing, some into subway stations, others into manholes. Six people were dead; another fifteen were seriously wounded. The attackers, the news said, used their teeth.

Teeth.

Subway.

It *was* a fucking cult. Or the world's strangest terror cell. Jesus Christ, what was happening in New York?

Chapter Ten

Harvey Goldblum sat numb before the television. The anchors went through the litany of horrors once more, their faces stoic and unaffected. Nine dead, twelve hurt.

It was noon, and sitting in the sun-washed living room overlooking Long Island Sound, the rising skyscrapers of New York City but a distant suggestion, Harvey Goldblum raised his hand to his mouth.

The people, the newscasters said, came from the subways. Witnesses described them as pale with dark eyes and long, pointed teeth, pointed teeth they used in place of knives and bombs. He hadn't heard the word "vampire" mentioned yet, but he was sure—no, he was *certain* —that that's what they were. Vampires. He thought back to the prostitute he read about in the paper, the one whose throat had been ripped out several days ago. The article made mention of a subway station. Whether it was close by or witnesses saw someone flee into it, he couldn't remember, but it *did* play a role.

So there were vampires.

Under New York City.

In his long career hunting the supernatural elements of America, Harvey had never come across hard proof that vampires existed, but he spoke with people who had been attacked, with holy men who claimed to have staked ghouls in their graves. When he was younger, he disbelieved such fantastic talk. Ghosts he could buy, but *vampires?* Reanimated corpses rising from their graves in search of blood? As he grew older, however, his mind opened. He saw great and terrible things. Stood at the bedside of a girl possessed by a demon, watched as she broke her own neck and then flopped it bonelessly back and forth, all the while singing satanic rock songs. "Hell's Bells." "Shout at the Devil." Watched as a black mist seeped through a solid stone wall and took the form of a creature with wide, gaping eyes and laughed at his and a medium's terror.

Demons, he decided long ago, were real. They nested in the shadows of abandoned houses, in the corners of nursing homes and mental hospitals, wherever, in fact, people suffered and died. A demonologist he once knew named Curtis Porter told him that demons fed upon the fear and pain of the living. He called them *Bodachs*, a sort of bogeyman originating in Gaelic folklore.

If demons exist and can possess the living, he figured, *why disbelieve vampires?*

Presently, he shook his head. In the bright noon sun, the notion seemed silly, even to a believer like him, but the evidence was strong, both for the existence of vampires and for them being the culprit in last night's assault on New York. Getting up from the couch, wearing only a long, silken robe, Harvey crossed the hardwood floor and stood at the French Doors opening onto the terrace. Beyond, past the yard and the steely blue waters of the Sound, New York sat clustered, looking as though it were nothing more than a painting on a backdrop.

He had to go into the city.

He had to stop this.

Chapter Eleven

Frank Burger woke at one in the afternoon, his head aching and his eyes stinging at the light falling through the window. After a hot shower and several cups of coffee, he phoned the precinct and asked for either Steve Johnson or Deke Meyers, the detectives who took over the case after Leary placed him on leave.

He got Meyers.

"Hey, Frank," Meyers said when he came on the line. "How are you doing?"

"I'm good," Frank croaked, though in actuality, he felt like shit. "I don't wanna be off, you know?" Frank honestly didn'tknow *what* he wanted.

Except to find the subway killers.

"Yeah," Dave said. "I don't think you'd wanna be around right now. It's crazy."

Frank could hear it. In the background, phones rang, people shouted. "I figured. I saw the news last night."

Meyers was silent for a moment. "Yeah," he finally said. "Terrible."

"Sounds a lot like the case we —"

"Valerie Baldwin and Donald Atkins," Meyers said immediately.

"That's it," he said, his heart clutching.

"You wanna hear something funny?" Meyers asked. From his tone, Frank could ascertain that what he was going to say would not be funny at all.

"What?"

"Baldwin's body went missing last night."

Frank blinked. "What?"

"Someone stole her body from the coroner's office. He came in this morning and she was gone."

Frank nearly dropped the phone.

"Frank? You there?"

"Yeah. I gotta go."

He sat the phone aside and laid back.

When he trusted himself, he left the apartment. Outside, the sun was bright and warm. At a corner market, he bought a newspaper and a bottle of cheap wine, then returned home. Sitting at the breakfast bar separating the living room from the kitchen, he read the reports of the previous night's horrors, and then, getting a pen and a pad of paper, he began to write.

Chapter Twelve

Harvey Goldblum drove into the city on the Northern State Parkway, the tomblike skyscrapers across the East River coming slowly into view like approaching giants. As he navigated through the outlying boroughs, he noticed a heavy police presence. At one point he even saw an olive green personnel carrier parked in the parking lot of an abandoned building, several soldiers standing around. National Guard, he thought, though he couldn't be sure.

Crossing the river over the Queensborough Bridge, he counted nearly a half dozen helicopters flying over the city, tiny silvery specks on a blue canvas. The evident display of force unnerved Harvey. It meant the city government was scared.

From the bridge, he turned south and followed Roosevelt Parkway toward Lower Manhattan, passing through Midtown East, Kips Bay, Gramercy Park, and the East Village. He got off the FDR at East Houston Street and parked in a lot next to an abandoned meatpacking plant. Leaving the engine on, the music a faint whisper, he pulled out his notepad and read what he had written. Two days ago, a woman named Valerie Baldwin was killed near a subway station, her throat ripped out. The only witness was an Iraqi man who owned a dry cleaning business. Before leaving the house, Harvey looked up the address of his business. It was several blocks northwest—across the street from a subway station.

Harvey backed the car into the street and headed north. On the short ride, he saw a number of uniformed police officers patrolling the streets. A radio newsbreak had said officers and National Guardsmen were going through the tunnels in search of the culprits. Harvey shuddered as he thought of what would become of those men; those fools wouldn't believe what they were seeing even as the vampires latched onto their necks.

Muhammad Atwarh's dry cleaning business was on the right side of the road, wedged between a butcher shop and a narrow gravel lane terminating in a chain-link fence. Harvey pulled into the alley and killed the engine. He got out, shivering at the chill—with skyscrapers blocking the light of the sun, the heart of Manhattan was *always* colder than Long Island—and opened the back driver's side door. He grabbed his bag, unzipped it, and pulled out a large crucifix supporting a silver Christ rendered in horrible detail: His face contorted in agony, blood spilling down His face from the thorny crown atop His head. Also in the bag were several stakes, a mallet, and a plastic two-liter bottle of holy water. He left everything but the cross: He doubted he would need even that, but being in such close proximity, he felt better with it.

Holding the cross at his side, Harvey circled around to the front of the building. An OPEN sign hung in the door. Rehearsing what he was going to say, he opened the door and stepped in.

Thick shadows filled the room. The front half of the shop, Harvey saw, was divided from the back by a long counter. Beyond that, shirts and pants hung from hangers.

"Hello?" Harvey called.

He waited a minute, expecting to hear someone approaching. When he didn't, he walked up to the counter. "Hello?"

Nothing.

Unconsciously gripping the cross tighter, Harvey went through the little opening between the wall and the edge of the counter. A short hall opened off the back room. "Hello?"

Harvey's heart was beating faster now. He started down the hall, holding the cross out in front of him like a talisman.

The hall ended at a door. Harvey reached out, turned the knob, his heart slamming, and opened it.

Total darkness. Harvey felt for a light switch, found it, and flipped it.

A man was lying on the floor next to a bed, his arms folded over his chest. Atop the bed, a woman reposed in a similar manner.

Harvey swallowed. "Hello?"

The woman sat up, and Harvey's heart leaped into his throat.

He recognized her from the paper.

Valerie Baldwin.

Her eyes were black, her face pale and drawn; when she opened her mouth, a long, rattling hiss issued forth.

The man sat up now, too.

Harvey was frozen.

Couldn't move.

Even though he suspected vampires, seeing them before him, in the flesh… Harvey closed his eyes and shook his head. *No.*

When he opened them, the man was standing, his arms limp at his sides. The woman rose from the bed, seeming to move without bending any of her joints, and stepped down to the floor, blocking the man. She hissed.

His fear unlocking, Harvey thrust the cross out in front of him. With a scream, the vampires shrank back, clawing and swatting. Shaking now, absolutely trembling, he backed out of the room, bumping into the doorjamb, and down the hall. The vampires followed, cautious, spitting and mewling like wild animals. When Harvey reached the counter, he went around and into a bar of sunshine falling through the window.

Still they came.

They were behind the counter now.

Harvey fumbled for the door, opened it, and stepped out, never once lowering the cross.

Only when he was back in his own car, safe with the doors locked, did he break down, his body convulsing and his teeth chattering. Pain flared in his chest, snaked down his arm, and he realized that he was having a heart attack.

First gray, then black, the world drew away from Harvey Goldblum...

... and never returned.

Chapter Thirteen

He stood high upon a stage. Below, the mewling denizens of his subterranean hell hissed and watched, all ears, all teeth.

"Tonight," he said, raising his arms. "Tonight, we take the city!"

An eerie cheer went up.

And Mr. Sewer Man was pleased.

By this time tomorrow, Manhattan would belong to the vampires.

Chapter Fourteen

At dusk, Frank Burger left his apartment and drove south through the streets of Manhattan. He was going back to where it all began, back to where, he suspected, it would begin again tonight: the subway station.

Passing Atwarh's shop, Frank pulled an illegal U-turn and parked at the curb. The stairs descending into the underworld were straight ahead, and he had a clear view of everyone who came and went.

One by one, the streetlamps lining the block winked on, casting shadows onto the street. He glanced over at Atwarh's and noticed a car parked in the gravel drive flanking the south wall. Squinting, he thought it was a Kia. Maybe a Soul. For some reason, it struck him as odd.

As if drawn by the thought of his name, Atwarh emerged from the shop with a blonde woman. In the instant before they turned up the deserted sidewalk and started north, Frank could have sworn she looked exactly like Valerie Baldwin, though skinnier. He briefly considered following them, but decided against it. He wanted to be close to the subway in case any suspicious characters appeared.

Speaking of suspicious… That damn Kia. It obviously didn't belong to Atwarh, though he supposed it *could* belong to his lady friend. He had a funny feeling about it, though, and in his nearly twenty years on the force, he had learned to trust his feelings.

For the rest of the evening then, he divided his attention between the staircase and the Kia. At seven, he turned off the radio and switched on a portable police scanner. If anything strange was happening in the city, he wanted to know about it. The Dracula Killers, so dubbed by the press, were his responsibility. If nothing else, he owed it to Martha to stop the sons of bitches.

He wished Martha was with him now. God, how he missed her wisecracks, her voice, her presence.

"I think it's Mole People," he said now, imagining that she was in the seat next to him. "You know the stories. They live in the abandoned subway tunnels, attack whoever comes down there. People say they're feral."

Mole People were a fixture of city lore, right up there with alligators in the sewers. He remembered hearing stories as a kid about the people in the tunnels, how they'd been down there so long they had gone blind, their eyes a sightless milky white, how they could no longer speak, couldn't remember how to walk upright. Evolutionary throwbacks, someone called them once. Down there, in the dark, with only the crashing silence to keep them company, they lost the essence of humanity and became animals. Worse, they became *monsters*.

When he joined the force, a lot of the older cops told him stories of going down into the tunnels and confronting *things* that looked only vaguely human. The city tried to evict the homeless from the tunnels in the late 80s and early 90s, and many of the cops working when he started had been involved. Frank took their word as gospel, but as he grew older and more cynical, he dismissed those stories as legends. Now, he was a full-fledged believer again. Atwarh claimed the man who attacked Valerie Baldwin looked like an evil spirit, his skin pale and his eyes black. At first, they thought the perp was a simple junkie, but they were wrong. So wrong. It was a Mole Person, one who had probably been born in the tunnels. Frank shivered as he imagined being born and living his entire life in the damp darkness.

The police scanner crackled, bringing him out of his thoughts. Armed robbery in Hell's Kitchen, the dispatcher said. All available units, please respond. Frank threw the car into drive, but stopped when he remembered that he wasn't active. Putting it back in park, he sank into his seat and watched the stairway. A crush of people came up and spread out. He checked the timetable he printed off that afternoon, followed the twisty, colored lines, and found that yes, a train had just let off.

It surprised him that the trains were running today. He saw on the news that officers were searching the tunnels and assumed that all service would be suspended. Maybe in another city it would be, but not here in the Big Apple, the city that never sleeps. How much would the city lose if they shut down the subway for a day? A lot. That bastard Mayor Brandon would *never* go for that.

Frank sighed. He watched as the last of the massive group ascended the stairs, following a young man with his eyes. The man crossed the street and started down the sidewalk past Atwarh's shop. He looked normal enough, they all did... But that damn Kia.

Mind made up, Frank got out of the car, shivering against the chilly breeze, and crossed the street. Under his long coat, he wore a gun, a flashlight, and his badge; though he wasn't active, the badge would help smooth the way if he needed to. I'm a cop, see? Legit.

On the other side, slightly down from Atwarh's shop, Frank paused, looked around as though he were a criminal, and started toward the Kia, pausing again at its back end. He pulled out the flashlight, clicked it on, and shined in through the back window.

Save for a folded blanket, the back compartment was empty. Walking along the passenger's side, he shined the light into the back seat. Nothing. When he shined it into the front window, he jerked. A man was slumped behind the wheel, his head lolling against his shoulder.

Oh no.

Frank rounded the front end of the vehicle and opened the door, catching the man as he fell over and lowering him gently to the ground: He knew from the chill of his skin that the man was dead.

Shit.

Something fell out of the car then, and Frank shined his light on it. A duffle bag. It was then that he noticed the crucifix lying on the running board beneath the door. He picked it up and turned it over in his hands. The man must have known he was dying, so he reached for the comfort of the cross as death took him. It reminded Frank of a body he found when he was a patrolman. The guy was the lead singer of a rock band with a hit on the charts. His manager called the police for a wellness check because he hadn't seen him for several days, and when Frank entered the man's apartment, he found him sprawled in front of the bedroom door, his mouth crusted with green OD foam. A rosary was clutched in his outstretched hand. Many nights afterward Frank found himself thinking of the man. He knew it was coming, could feel his body shutting down, and the last thing he did was grab his rosary and pray as his vision darkened.

Sighing, Frank stuffed the cross into his jacket pocket, grabbed the bag, and unzipped it. What he found inside gave him pause: a dozen stakes, their business ends razor sharp; a wooden mallet; and a plastic bottle filled with water. What was this guy doing, hunting vampires?

Putting the bag back onto the driver's seat, he noticed a notebook lying on the passenger's seat. Leaning in, he picked it up and, half spinning, sat on the edge of the driver's seat:

VALERIE BALDWIN: ATTACKED AND KILLED JANUARY 26. THROAT RIPPED OUT. BITEMARKS.

JAN 27: ASSAILANTS COME OUT OF SUBWAYS AND ATTACK PEOPLE, BITING THEM. THEY ARE DESCRIBED AS PALE AND WITH BLACK EYES. VAMPIRES?

Frank looked up from the notebook, his mind racing. The dead man's face was revealed in a spill of moonlight. His soft features, his sensuous lips. He was old, in his sixties if not his seventies, and his hair was carrot red.

He thought actual vampires were behind yesterday's attack.

Frank would have laughed if he wasn't entirely sure the guy wasn't wrong. He remembered the cell phone footage from the Atkins murder. Everything was clear as day except the attackers. They were invisible.

Vampires?

Looking back down at the notebook, he found Atwarh's address. So he drove out here and... What? Slipping off the seat and onto his knees, Frank checked the man for visible wounds, but found nothing. Maybe he had a stroke when he pulled up. It happened. A blood clot waits for no man. He found that out when his father fell down dead after mowing the lawn: He came in, sat down in his chair, and that was it.

Only Frank didn't think it happened that way. This guy, whatever his name was, didn't simply die. Maybe he saw something and it pushed him into a heart attack. Maybe Atwarh fed him a poisoned scone.

Shaking his head, Frank stood, shoved the notebook into the bag, and slung the bag over his shoulder. Next, he hefted the man back into the car and closed the door: He was crammed in an unnatural position. He would call the police later, he told himself as he started back toward the street; right now, he didn't want a bunch of activity. He...

A scream cut the night.

Heart rocketing into his throat, Frank ran to the sidewalk just in time to see a woman explode from the staircase to the subway and dart south. Seconds later, a mass of people flooded out. In the light of a strategically placed streetlamp, Frank could see their faces, not clearly but well enough to know that something was off about them, not right.

Instinctively, Frank fell back a step and crouched alongside the Kia. He raised his head just enough to see them with little chance of them seeing him back.

A tall man broke from the crowd, gesturing wildly with one arm. "Come!" he screamed, his cold voice echoing off the buildings around. "Let us take the city!"

Striding with purpose, like a general at the head of a grand army, the man stalked off to the left, disappearing from sight. A hissing cheer went up among his troops and they spread out, filling the street and heading in every direction. Several of them crossed to Frank's side of the street and streamed past him, affording a clear view of their faces. He saw with a twist of the stomach that they were pale, skeletal.

The Mole People.

Beginning to panic—and hating himself for it—Frank searched his pockets for his cell phone, but it wasn't there. Then he remembered that he left it in the car, and damned himself as an idiot. A good cop never leaves his only mode of communication in the car.

Poking his head up, he saw that the street before him was empty. Withdrawing his gun, he stood and darted across the street, glancing both ways as he did. The Mole People were nowhere in sight, though he could hear screaming and honking horns in the distance.

Just when he reached the driver's side door, a man came up from the stairs, making moaning and hissing noises. Blood running cold, Frank turned. He was a big man, white or Hispanic, and breathed heavily, his frame rising and falling.

"You..." he hissed, and started forward.

Frank raised the gun. "Freeze!"

Cackling, the man continued his advance.

"Freeze!" Frank screamed again, suddenly feeling very small and weak.

The man kept coming.

Frank squeezed off three quick shots, aiming at the man's torso. It was textbook. Perfect. But the man didn't fall. He didn't even slow.

Verging on hysteria, Frank aimed for his head. The man was fifteen feet away. He fired. *Saw* the bullet enter above the right eye, saw the mist of blood and brain matter fly from the back of his head. But still, he kept coming.

Impossible!

Frank jerked the door open, mindlessly shoving the gun into his pocket. He climbed into the car, slammed the door, and locked it just as the man reached him, ripping at the handle. His face was less than a foot away then, and in that terrible moment, Frank knew that the man wasn't alive, and hadn't been the whole time. He was pale, waxy, his eyes shining liquid black. He pulled his lips back over his teeth, and Frank saw the fangs.

No. No!

The man stepped back from the window and kicked the side of the door.

The cross!

Frank fumbled in his pocket, didn't feel it, nearly screamed with frustration, then found it. Ripping it out, he slapped it against the window. The man, so tall and broad before, seemed to deflate when he saw the holy object. Screaming, he fell back a step and threw his hands up like a man protecting himself from a blast of burning light.

Holding the cross against the window, Frank turned the key, threw the car into DRIVE, and rocketed off, spinning the wheel sharply to the right to avoid plowing into a streetlamp. Dropping the cross into his lap and looking back, Frank saw the creature standing in the middle of the street, its arms at its sides.

Breathing heavy, Frank took a right up ahead, passing a taxi, and then another right.

When he saw them, he hit the brakes.

They were running through the streets, on the sidewalks, like children unleashed on the most irresistible playground ever built. They smashed windows, overturned cars, broke down doors. In the headlights, they looked like demons, finally free from hell and set upon the world for a night-long feast.

One of them, bent over the broken body of a man, looked up, its face gray and its eyes reflecting the light like a cat, and got stiffly to its feet.

Others left what they were doing and started for him, some running, some ambling.

Someone screamed as Frank threw the car into reverse. He didn't realize it was him.

Angling slightly to the right, he slammed into a newspaper dispenser. He put the car into DRIVE just as they reached him, throwing themselves on the hood, their dead faces mashed against the windshield. Still screaming, Frank hit the gas and shot across the street, clipping a traffic light as he went. Some of the vampires fell off, but one held on, gnashing its teeth at him through the windshield. He lifted one fist and smashed it against the glass, cracking it.

Unthinking, his mind a blur of panic, Frank grabbed the gun and fired. The bullet hit the thing in the head and flung it over the side. He looked in the rearview mirror and saw them, bathed in the red glow of the taillight, running after him.

Jerking the wheel hard to the right, he turned onto Pitt Street. To his right, several apartment buildings rose up into the night, blotting out the stars. A few figures darted across the street ahead of him. He looked in the mirror again. The vampires were no longer behind him.

Letting out a breath he didn't know he was holding, Frank turned onto Delancey Street, a narrow through lane flanking a stone wall supporting the Williamsburg Bridge. Ahead, a car sat with both doors open and its engines running. Wincing, he threw the car into reverse and turned left on Ridge Street, which passes under the bridge. Several cars sat empty, their doors standing open and their taillights glowing in the darkness. He pulled up onto the sidewalk and eased past them. Ahead, people ran to and fro in the shadows of tall buildings. He couldn't see if they were vampires or not.

Just then, a rock hit the windshield.

Chapter Fifteen

Mr. Sewer Man was pleased with the chaos around him.

Whistling and twirling a cane in his right hand, he strolled along 1st Avenue, a broad street boasting an assortment of shops, restaurants, and storefronts. His forces ran rampant through the streets, dragging people out their cars and breaking into their homes and places of business. Screaming, breaking glass, and alarm bells scented the frosty air. Somewhere, someone opened fire, and tires squealed. Many cars blocked the avenue, and people farther back honked their horns in frustration at the delay, not knowing what was happening.

He smiled widely. Everything was going according to plan. At precisely 8:05 p.m., ten thousand vampires had poured into the city, coming up from every nook, cranny, and crevice on the island. Two teams were in Jersey, and another in Staten Island. Soon, when Manhattan was paralyzed, they would cross the bridges into Brooklyn, Queens, and Yonkers.

It was going to be a *long* night.

For the mortals.

Chapter Sixteen

The vampire punched through the driver's side window and reached in, its fingers long and claw-like. Frank smacked the creature with the crucifix. It screamed and fell back. Frank punched the gas.

Two blocks south, Frank clipped the ass end of a taxi, knocking it aside. As he staggered away on foot, he thought that his head had hit the steering wheel, but he wasn't sure. All he knew was that he was bleeding.

Screaming, gunfire, and the hot tang of smoke filled the air.

At Grand Street, he turned left, following a wrought iron fence toward the FDR Drive, and then realized he was passing a Catholic church.

He ducked through the gate and went inside.

Chapter Seventeen

Mayor Ray Brandon sat stiffly behind his desk, his eyes far away. Outside, three dozen NYPD officers guarded city hall, supplemented by a dozen National Guardsmen.

City Hall is in a hilly, grassy complex in Lower Manhattan, virtually at the foot of the Brooklyn Bridge. The invasion began nearby, and now Brandon, dazed, could hear the symphony of terror: screaming, gunshots.

"We have a chopper on the way," Jerry Hinkel, the Chief of Police, said. A large man with glasses and a mustache, Hinkle looked afraid.

Brandon nodded, not knowing what Hinkel said. Like a robot, he stood and went to the window overlooking the common. Through the screen of trees along Park Row, he could see dark figures storming through the streets.

Brandon didn't know what the creatures loose in the city were. Ghouls. Zombies. Vampires. Something…something not human. Hinkel told him that the NYPD's bullets had no effect on them. Madness, he thought.

Brandon's heart stopped.

They were coming through the trees now, a dozen, a hundred, invading the common. Someone yelled for them to freeze, but they kept advancing, slow and steady, sure of themselves.

Then the shooting started. Small arms fire. A few shotguns. M4s carried by the Guardsmen rattled. Brandon closed the curtain and looked at Hinkel, the latter's eyes wide with fright. "It's the end," Brandon mumbled. He sat down, not quite remembering *why* it was the end, but knowing that it was here at last. He opened a drawer, removed a pearl-handled pistol, and put it to his head. Before Hinkel could even scream for him to stop, he pulled the trigger.

Chapter Eighteen

A line of police officers, many of them brought in from Queens, formed along the Bowery, east of the NYU campus and north of East Houston Street. They were equipped with handguns, riot gear, shotguns, and a few assault rifles from the SWAT division. They stood shoulder-to-shoulder across the street, behind cruisers and yellow sawhorses. They were nervous, afraid. "Fuck this," one of them said, and deserted.

Shortly before ten, a massive group of people appeared at the end of the street. Everything south of them was lost. Fires burned, alarms rang unchecked, and the occasional gunshots had died away twenty minutes before.

"Hold the line!" Captain Gus Harris yelled as the army began marching down the street. Harris was terrified. He could hear them hissing and spitting. He'd heard over the radio how bullets couldn't stop them. He knew they took City Hall from nearly forty cops and an entire National Guard unit. Still, it was his duty to protect New

York City, and if he was going to die, he was going to die fighting.

When the first rank emerged from the shadows and into the bright floodlights set up behind the line of demarcation, Harris's heart dropped into his stomach. They were white-faced, black-eyed, lumbering like zombies. A few cops broke and ran then. Harris couldn't blame them.

"Fire!" he yelled.

A cannonade erupted as a hundred guns went off simultaneously, reverberating through the city. Shotguns. M4s. A few Uzis and fully auto AK47's raided from the evidence lockers.

Still they came.

When they were five feet from the cars parked nose-to-nose across the street, the line faltered, and the rest of Harris's men fled.

Grabbing a fallen AK47, Harris raked the first row with gunfire, aiming high, hitting a dozen heads.

Still they came on, and Gus Harris died defending New York City.

Chapter Nineteen

Across town, the men of Firehouse #10, FDNY, all devout Catholics, patrolled the streets between the FDR Drive and Park Ave South. They drove tankers only, and stopped to open every hydrant they came across. Joey O'Donnell was the one who first mentioned the word "vampire," and though the other guys laughed nervously, they got Father Thomas Mackey from nearby St. George's to come with them and bless as much water as he could.

At 9:50, they encountered a line of ghouls pushing north through the narrow residential streets. Chief Joshua Magin, a tall man with a thick white mustache, called for his men to aim and fire. Jesse Sturgis, manning the water cannon, aimed at the advancing ghouls and pulled the trigger.

When the water hit them, a chorus of howls rose into the night, accompanied by the terrible sizzle of dead flesh burning from dead bone.

"Holy shit," Sturgis whispered. The ghouls fell back and fled.

"Holy water!" Magin cried into the radio. "Get every goddamn priest you can find and bless *everything!*"

Chapter Twenty

The first National Guard troops to enter New York City after the "mass unrest" began came from the north via New Rochelle and Yonkers, the 5th Mounted Division. They sailed through the night along I-95, a fleet of Humvees, Stryker personnel carriers—the men called them "Gators" because they looked like alligators—and support vehicles. Once in the city, they were strung out in a rough battle line from the FDR Drive in the east and the Henry Hudson Parkway in the west, the line passing along the southern flank of Central Park. They were given strict orders to hold the line at all costs, to protect Fifth Avenue and the fashionable Upper West Side with their very lives. The men called it "bullshit."

"They got us protecting all the rich people," Pvt. James Matheson said. He was short, skinny, and black; he looked tiny behind the massive .50 caliber M2 mounted to the roof of a Humvee. "What about down there?" He nodded south. The sounds were faint but present: alarm bells, shooting, screaming.

At 11:22 p.m., they were supplemented by an FDNY tanker. Col. Richard Potter, the commander, listened tightly as the men explained the situation.

"Vampires?" he barked when they were done. They were in his tent, pitched among the tall trees and still ponds dotting the southeastern edge of Central Park.

"I know it sounds crazy, Colonel," Josh Magin said, "but I saw it with my own two eyes."

Sighing, Potter said, "Fine."

He ordered one of his subordinates to raid several of the toy stores north of the line. By 12:05 a.m., they had fifty-eight Super Soakers. Father Mackey blessed the water, even hitting the ponds in the park, and Potter handed them out to his men, feeling like the biggest fool on the face of the earth.

"Take this seriously!" Magin cried when he saw some of the men tittering. "Unless you wanna wind up like Battery Park!"

That shut them up.

Chapter Twenty-One

By 12:30 a.m., all of Manhattan south of West 47th Street was completely overrun. But while the streets belonged to the living dead, a number of people had barricaded themselves in their apartments, businesses, and in public bathrooms, storerooms, etc. Crosses appeared on doors, on windows, drawn with pen, pencil, marker, and whatever else was available, and the vampires were powerless to enter.

Mr. Sewer Man knew this, but didn't care. A few peasants hiding in toilets didn't concern him. It was the soldiers strung out along West 57th Street that worried him. Standing in the middle of a street teeming with more vampires than he could count, many of them new converts, he raised his hands and yelled "North! North!"

He stormed down the street, crunching glass underfoot, ducked around an overturned SUV, and motioned for his people to follow him. They had to act fast. If they didn't, they would lose the element of surprise.

Chapter Twenty-Two

Frank Burger found the church empty. Candles burned on the altar, providing a soft light, but when he searched, he found that he was completely and utterly alone.

Dropping into a pew before the altar with a sigh, Frank listened to the chaos around him. Screaming, wailing, gunfire, crashing cars, running feet on the sidewalks.

Remembering his cell phone, he took it out of his pocket and placed a call to Captain Leary at the 17th Precinct.

He answered on the fifth ring. "Leary."

"It's Frank Burger," Frank said, and realized his voice shook.

"Burger, this is a bad time ..."

"They're vampires."

Leary was quiet a moment. "What'd you say? Vampires?"

Frank nodded. "I know it sounds crazy, but they're vampires. Guns don't work on them, but crosses and holy water do."

"That's crazy, Burger."

"*I know, goddamn it!*" Frank yelled, surprised at the fury rising in his chest. "I just plowed through fifteen blocks worth of them. I shot one in the head, and he didn't even slow down. If you let the boys use guns, they're dead, and their blood is on *your* hands." His voice broke. "Crosses and holy water!"

He clicked the END button and listened to his voice echoing in the vaulted eaves. He wished Martha was with him. He missed her so much.

With that, he curled into a ball and cried.

Chapter Twenty-Three

By 1:00 a.m., troops were stationed at each bridge going into Manhattan. People who saw them swore they were regular army. There was one odd thing about them: They carried bright yellow and green water guns instead of rifles.

West New York, across the Hudson from the city, was the site of several attacks, but by 10:00 it was over, the half-dozen vampires killed by a group of civilian survivalists with an ordained minister among their rank.

A dozen attacks occurred across northern Staten Island between 7:00 p.m. and 9:00 p.m., the first in West New Brighton and the last in Park Hill. Why they stopped is a mystery.

Chapter Twenty-Four

Mr. Sewer Man halted his troops. Ahead, fifty yards away, the Avenue of Americans met West 57th Street. A rank of soldiers stood at the ready.

"On!" he screamed.

When they were fifty feet from the intersection, he saw the five red fire trucks. "Halt!" he yelled.

The mass didn't listen; they shoved past him, lost in the grip of bloodlust. When the cannons opened up and the water struck them, they screamed and fell back, hissing and sizzling.

"Retreat!" he screamed, and the tide turned, fleeing all the way back to Times Square.

Chapter Twenty-Five

"They're on the run," Potter said into the radio.

"Hold your position," the Defense Department replied.

Potter sighed. He pulled a cigar from his pocket and sniffed it, relishing the grape-like scent. Then he plopped it into his mouth and lit it. It was 1:35 a.m.

Chapter Twenty-Six

They would never get past, Mr. Sewer Man realized with a flash of anger. Everything north of West 57th Street was closed to them. Thinking fast, he divided his army into three regiments. One would split up and cross the East River, one through the Queens-Midtown Tunnel, and the other through the river itself. One would remain at Times Square. The third would move west to 9th Avenue. If they attacked from two fronts, he realized, maybe they could scare the humans into a retreat.

The first regiment struck off. The one passing through the tunnel was met with an army unit coming into the city; they were fired upon by water cannons and were forced to retreat. The second front was decimated at the water. Some monster had blessed it, and nearly a hundred of his number were lost when they leaped thoughtlessly in.

"Come on!" he screamed. This was it. His last stand. They would break through the 57th line, or they would die trying.

Chapter Twenty-Seven

At 1:40 a.m., the invasion began.

Army vehicles equipped with water cannons began moving into the city through the Holland Tunnel, the Lincoln Tunnel, the Queens-Midtown Tunnel, and over the Brooklyn Bridge. The commander of the operation, General Ken McAllister, watched from Jersey as the first vehicles crept into Downtown. Through his binoculars, he could see them encountering little to no resistance. Per Col. Potter, most of the vampires were just south of his line, in Times Square. A chopper confirmed that at 1:38 a.m. "There's gotta be a million of 'em down there!" the pilot screamed.

At 1:39 a.m., McAllister radioed McGuire AFB. "Send the copters," he said.

By 1:41 a.m., fifteen helicopters were soaring through the night, each one loaded with enough holy water to drown a nation of vampires. They were under orders to drop water only on Times Square and points north, but south of the 57th Line.

The war is won. McAllister smiled.

Chapter Twenty-Eight

"Charge!"

Mr. Sewer Man led his force up the Avenue of the Americans. The water cannons fired. Vampires screamed. A spray hit him in the face, and he howled as it ate the soft flesh of his cheeks like acid.

In agony, he ducked into a doorway and fell to his knees. The pressure of the water knocked vampires to the ground, where the sheer amount of water reduced them to ash.

It was then that he heard the choppers.

Looking up, he panicked, for he knew what they signified; he watched as, one-by-one, they dropped their loads.

In the last moment before the water consumed him, he hoped his people on 9th Avenue fared better.

Chapter Twenty-Nine

They did.

But not by much.

The sole fire engine on that side malfunctioned, and the vampires were briefly able to overrun 57th Street. For five glorious minutes, they ran rampant up Central Park West, past the ancient brownstones overlooking the park. Then another tanker showed up, and a helicopter from New Jersey dropped its load.

Then it was over.

Chapter Thirty

Frank Burger woke to soft orange light streaming through the narrow windows under the eaves. Sitting up in the pew, his back and neck sore, it took him a few minutes to realize that silence prevailed over the city. The horrible sounds of the night before were gone, replaced by the fresh, clean sound of birds chirruping in the trees.

It was daylight.

The vampires were gone.

Outside, on the wide stone steps fronting the street, Frank surveyed the city: Over a chain-link fence and through a nest of dead trees, he could see the sun-dappled East River. Trash fluttered along the street, pushed by a hollow wind blowing through the urban canyons. Glass twinkled on the pavement. Thin brown smoke puffed into the sky from the north.

Clutching the crucifix to his chest, Frank walked east, toward the FDR Drive. The silence lying over the city was preternatural, disquieting. Did they win?

The first signs of life he saw were flashes of vehicles crossing the Brooklyn Bridge. Then the roar of helicopters sailing overhead from the direction of Long Island.

On the FDR Drive, cars sat abandoned at weird angles, littering the way like toys dropped by a giant toddler in the midst of an epic meltdown.

He saw others then, moving carefully through the wreckage like him, dazed and shell-shocked. Frank stood in the middle of the street until the first convoy reached him, an armored column of desert-tan Jeeps and Humvees. A man sat behind the gun affixed to the roof of the lead Humvee, his eyes hidden by a pair of sunglasses.

The convoy slowed, stopped.

"State you identity!" the man behind the gun barked.

"Frank Burger," Frank said, the meeting so surreal he grinned. "NYPD."

"Have you been bitten?"

Frank shook his head.

"Get in. There's a refugee center in Central Park."

Refugee center? Frank thought as they followed the FDR Drive, passing the destruction. In America?

He shook his head.

Strange times.

Strange times indeed.

GRAVE MARKER

A.P. SESSLER

THE
FIRST SUITOR

Chapter One

As the last of the wedding guests pulled out of the long, red brick driveway, Howie walked hand-in-hand with Elise up the tall stone staircase to the front door of her (now their) hilltop manor. He looked up with near-dizzying awe from the front porch landing to Sallow Manor's towering spires as they reached for the edge of the sky like fevered fingers longing to pull the cool sheet of night over itself and the setting sun. Turn around and gazing down across the lawn, the manor's shadow covered the hillside, the long phantom spires clawing at the foot of Willow Hill as though digging their own grave.

The door creaked open.

"Greetings, Reggie," said Elise to the waxy-skinned man.

His slick black hair was parted down the middle atop his egg-white face. Only his cracked, pink lips had any hint of color, and with the exception of his white dress shirt, he dressed entirely in black.

He quietly held the door until Elise and Howie passed through.

Upon first inspection, the new groom found the open-ceiling foyer just as dizzying to behold as the manor's outside view. The room featured a large, sparkling crystal chandelier that could have easily held Howie's attention for minutes if not for the servants coming and going. A hand-carved railing and crab apple-green carpet lined the wood staircase, spiraling upward to the second-story landing. The railing continued along the balcony walkway. Three doors were visible from where he stood: one at either end of the hall, and one between.

Another servant passed before Howie.

"I've never seen so many men in monkey suits," he said.

"Beg pardon?" Elise asked with a raised brow.

He waved his hand at another passing man. "All these waiters."

"You mean *servants*. As you will soon learn, those with wealth don't waste it on mere possessions."

"I never imagined spending it on anything else," Howie said, giving the foyer a second look.

"Oh, Howard."

"You know I hate my name. It sounds like an old man."

"Howie is a boy's name."

"I'm okay with that," he said, passing by her to look at a sheathed sword mounted on an end table beside the staircase. He unsheathed the ringing blade with childlike admiration and held it over his head so that it caught the light from the crystal chandelier.

"Trust me, darling," said Elise, offering Reggie an arm to remove her mink stole. "You are moving up in the world. You may have despised your name growing up, but your parents named you so because they knew you were made for big things. You have thought too small for too long. I shall make you a big man, my dear."

Reggie placed the stole on a coat rack by the door.

Howie felt a cold hand on his shoulder, so cold it penetrated his wedding jacket and the shirt beneath. He turned his head to find Reggie behind him, ready to remove his outer garment as well. "I'm fine, thank you," he told the servant.

The cold hand remained on his shoulder.

"No, really. I'm fine. Thank you."

The cold hand slid off his shoulder the way runny mud falls off an automobile tire when it comes to a halt. Reggie left the room without a word.

Howie sheathed the sword and approached Elise from behind. He ran his hands down her back to her hips. "Does that mean I have to use lots of big words?" he said in her ear.

"Nonsense, darling," she said with a smile, enjoying his slow caress. "Big words or an abundance of them don't prove the man—they only test the patience of those who must listen. Big thoughts produce big actions, and I know you're cut from the right cloth. After all, you did choose me," she said, turning to face him. She nuzzled the dimple of his stubbled chin with her slender nose and pressed her lips against his.

He took her arms in his strong grasp, unintentionally pulling the loose half sleeves of her silk dress past her shoulders. At the sight of her own naked collarbone, she elicited an anxious gasp.

He inhaled her breath like some fresh herb or flower. He kissed her again, and before she knew what was happening, he swept her off her, and she lay cradled in his arms. With another anxious gasp, schoolgirl butterflies stirred in her stomach and he carried her up the winding staircase toward the bedroom that now was theirs.

Though cautiously mindful of every step, he stared into her dark, longing eyes. He blindly fiddled at the brass door handle, unable to turn it. She laughed like a woman drunk with wine, craning her neck forward as she, too, blindly reached for the door handle, but with more success than her lover.

He inhaled her fragrant laughter and tasted its source once more before nudging the door open with his foot and stepping over the threshold. Even when he pushed the door shut with his right foot, he didn't look away from her. When he gently laid her on their bed, the thick purple blankets slowly billowed up around her slender form like soft, dark clouds in luscious contrast to her moon-white flesh.

"Ravish me," she purred.

Outside the lovers' door, a silent servant ran a feather duster over a slender hourglass-shaped vase. He carried out his duties, paying no mind to their throes of passion.

Chapter Two

Howie's closed eyes flickered sloshed side to side. He licked his dry lips while the vivid dream continued. He sat at his drafting desk, staring at a blueprint, as an ink pen in his right hand dripped white ink from its tip onto the blueprint.

The next moment he stood outside on a sidewalk, staring across the street at the same blueprint, only it was the size of a city block. A stone fountain complete with spitting cherubim bubbled up from an abstract symbol on the blue surface, and around it walls protruded from white rectangular outlines to meet spreading ceilings that became floors. Paths stretched left and right, connected hall to hall via corners. Growing elevator shafts housed cars that would go from ground floor to penthouse. Intricately carved stone columns arose from the flat, outlined circles on the drawing and grew so high he couldn't see their tops. Lions lounged upon pedestals, standing guard on the porches, and stairs of equally glorious form sprung forth to the tower's entrance.

The creation was magnificent, and of his own design, even if it was something from the depths of his subconscious. He stood in breathless admiration of his work because he knew the moment he awoke the building would be no more than a few circles and rectangles of indiscriminate length and position, forgotten no matter how hard he tried to commit it to conscious memory.

He traced the shapes again and again with his finger, hoping they would be irrevocably gouged into his mind, an indelible mark on the soft gray folds of his brain. He stared at each curve and line, at each scalloped indenture among the columns. It was so beautiful he cried.

As he stood beneath the colossal work of art, the ground began to shake. He lowered his gaze to the giant blueprint beneath the building's foundation. Drawings he had not noticed before lined the blueprint's perimeter.

When he comprehended what they were, the paper tore with a loud ripping sound. Ferocious claws emerged, accompanied by black clouds of smoke and the unmistakable smell of sulfur. Hideous demons burst from beneath the blueprint and flew to the top of the building on great stone wings. The creatures ascended to their perches among the tower's ledges.

Stone gargoyles: the piece de resistance of any great architecture. But there was something different about their appearance. They didn't bow their heads in silent humility or shame; each turned its head in perfect unison to stare in the same direction—into the blinding sun quickly emerging from behind the building's west side.

Howie awoke. He turned his head to see a flash of lightning split the black night sky in two outside the bedroom window. During the long, strobing flash, he could see the sallow tree, every branch and leaf, as clear as if it were daylight.

He gazed at the tree long enough to ensure it had not been set aflame from the lightning strike. He waited for the crack of thunder that should have been instantaneous, but it never arrived, unless it occurred sometime after he fell back into his bed and the deepest, most ecstatic sleep he had ever experienced.

Chapter Three

After slowly wearing down his resolve to stay in bed all the day, the morning sunlight pried Howie's heavy eyelids open. Beams of light shone between the black, diamond-pattern muntin of their single bedroom window.

He sighed deeply and stared at the ceiling. *I'm married*, he thought. *Actually married*.

He rolled over to see the curve of Elise's shoulder. He followed the sun-gilded line to her bare back. She had warned him of her scars soon after they met, and he had seen them several times since. She had mentioned an abusive past, something she would not discuss. In truth, they were only skin deep, and the rest of her beauty made them pale by comparison. If that and the fact she was some twenty years older (or so he assumed) was all he had to worry about, then he had *nothing* to worry about.

He pulled aside the purple satin sheet and swung his legs over the edge of the bed. He hitched up his boxers around his waist, then searched for the rest of his clothes. He found them strewn from the foot of the bed to their private bath.

What a night, he thought. Even if that happened only once a month, he would be a happy man. When he unlocked the bedroom door, he heard her stir. He chose not to disturb her.

As he trotted down the steps, he glanced at the collection of oil portraits that ran parallel to the stair. Each featured a man in regal pose wearing the fashion of his time, dating back centuries. In between glimpses at the masterful portraits, he managed to force shirt buttons through their somewhat respective holes. He was so focused on the task at hand when he reached the bottom of the stairs that he nearly knocked down a servant.

"Sorry. Didn't see you there," Howie said to the man in chef's hat and apron. "Guess I should watch where I'm going."

The servant resembled Reggie in complexion and was equally as talkative. Howie pointed at the portraits with a thumb and finished buttoning his shirt. "These guys part of the royal family?" he asked.

The servant didn't even glance in Howie's direction.

"In a manner of speaking," Elise answered.

Howie looked up to see his wife, now dressed in a night robe, standing behind the balcony rail.

"Manny, would you see that breakfast is prepared?" she said, don-ning a set of pearl earrings. "Howard and I would like Eggs Benedict and three slices of toast, one for myself, two for him. We'd also like—"

"Actually," Howie said, interrupting her. "I'll take my eggs scrambled with—"

"Nonsense, Howard," she said, cutting him off while descending the stairs. "You're no longer living in your small country town, and you're certainly not eating food fit for fat truck drivers at some disgusting greasy spoon."

"But—" he started before being interrupted again.

"Trust me, Howard. I know what's best for you. Now how would you like your coffee?"

His jaws clenched in a silent tantrum.

"Howard? I asked you a question," she said.

"If I have a *choice*, I'd like it with lots of sugar and creamer."

While Howie was speaking, Manny faced his mistress.

She rolled her eyes and shook her head. "And do fix me a kettle of rosemary tea. Thank you, Manny. That is all."

Manny bowed his head and left for the kitchen.

"Oh, Howard," Elise said, coming to stand in front of her husband and placing her hands around his neck.

"What?" he asked, tense.

She straightened the back of his collar with a smile, then ran her hands over his chest. She began unbuttoning his shirt from top to bottom.

He looked at her hands, then at his own chest, and realized that despite his efforts he had misaligned each of his shirt's buttons.

"I told you, Howard, I always know what's best."

He smirked and ran his left hand through her cropped, golden hair. He kissed her.

"Come," she said. "Let's have a seat in the dining room."

Chapter Four

Breakfast was pleasant. The bay room where they dined sat right of the kitchen. The small, round table was covered with a red-and-white checkered cloth, while the wood spindled chairs they sat on were certainly more formal. Behind Elise and opposite Howie, the large window let all the morning sun pour in.

Though Howie smarted over her gastronomical veto, he did feel more like a real man of the world, eating his "grown-up" eggs. Still, before he dared apply butter to his toast, he eyed Elise for her approval. She smiled and took another bite of toast lightly smeared with raspberry jam.

He applied a generous portion of butter to a slice; not as generous as he would have liked, but probably more than she approved of. He immediately faced the decision of which fruit spread he should choose, if any. Raspberry jam or orange marmalade? He glanced at Elise, her head bowed to take a bite of Eggs Benedict followed by a sip of tea.

He took a clean spoon and placed into one of the two small opened jars before him. Orange marmalade it was. He plopped the orange glob onto his toast and spread it out; the tiny slivers of orange rind spaced evenly across the crusty, golden surface. It may have been a small victory, but choosing the jam without her consent softened the earlier blow to his ego.

"Last night was wonderful," she said.

He nearly choked on the sweet mouthful when he noticed a servant standing between him and the china cabinet. The servant's blond Mod haircut looked plastered to his head, far more fitting of a British Invasion pop star, and the Adam's apple on his thin neck stuck out unusually far from Howie's perspective. Howie involuntarily sneered when he gazed up the man's hairless nose.

"Never mind Phil. He's not interested what happens behind closed doors, and certainly not our sex life," she said, then finished her piece of toast.

Howie watched Phil for a reaction. When none followed he spoke softly. "I should be thanking you. I've never—"

She cleared her throat, immediately silencing him, and rubbed the side of her bottom lip.

"What?" Howie whispered, then glanced back at Phil.

"No, dear," she said, regaining his attention. She took her cloth napkin and reached across the table to wipe the corner of his mouth.

She sat back in her chair and folded the napkin. "You were saying?"

He sighed. "You're welcome."

She pushed the empty plate aside and smiled, then finished her tea with a final swallow. Phil took the copper kettle from a large, ceramic tile placed at the center of the table and poured its steaming contents into her cup. He returned the kettle to the coaster and removed the dirty plate.

She gingerly raised the china cup and inhaled the vapors. Howie caught a whiff of the aromatic tea.

"That—" He refrained from using the word "smells." "—is interesting. What is that again?" "Black tea with rosemary, and a few other herbs," she said, then took a careful sip. She returned the cup to its saucer. "I like to keep the names simple for the help. They're quite familiar with all my recipes by now. If you care to try any, they are in the food pantry, each labeled by content and use."

"Your tea has multiple uses? I assume they're all for *drinking*, correct?"

"Don't be silly, Howard, of course they're for drinking, but each herb is used to achieve different ends, and all are very sacred to me."

"What would some of those *ends* be?"

"Healing, vitality, protection, favor, or something as simple as a good night's sleep."

"The herbal thing—isn't that part of your religion?"

With a look of surprise, her back went stiff. "Yes, which along with politics is something we don't discuss while dining."

"I apologize."

Her eyes returned to her saucer. "You're still learning," she said, then took another sip of tea. "Now what would you like to do today?"

He sat back in the chair and ran his fingers through his hair. Her brow furrowed when she observed the action. "I dunno," he answered. "I guess I could start the masterpiece that'll make me the big man you want me to be."

"Nonsense, Howard. We're still on our honeymoon. Why not go out for some fresh air? See the property, meet the help."

He stood up and pushed the chair back, then circled the table and kissed her on the cheek. "I guess I could do that, if I can hold off on being a big man for now."

She reached her hand between the top two buttons of his shirt and drew him close. "Last night you were all the big man you could ever be. And tonight we will have more of it."

Howie glanced around for Phil, but he had left the room. "I'll try not to exert myself during the walk. Be back after a while."

"Howard," she said.

"Yes?"

"Fetch a jacket. There's a chill outside."

"Yes—" He was about to say "ma'am," but caught himself, "—dear."

A moment later Howie stood in front of the coat rack, scanning its contents up and down several times. Among the items of clothing hung a dinner jacket, a winter jacket, and a heavy leather jacket, but nothing fall-friendly.

As he sifted through the rack, he felt a familiar cold hand upon his shoulder. Before Howie could turn around, Reggie had already pulled a sleeve over his right arm.

"Ah, I guess that's the kind of jacket I was looking for. Thanks. I can get it from here," Howie said, trying to pull the other sleeve from Reggie.

Reggie insisted he help Howie, even making his first audible objection known. No word was spoken, just a quick gasp of air. Howie couldn't tell if the asthmatic moan was inhaled or exhaled, but it unnerved him to the point of grabbing for the door handle and throwing the door open.

"Thank you, I'm fine, really," said Howie, pulling the sleeve from Reggie. He quickly closed the door, almost shutting it on Reggie's hand.

"Sorry, Reggie," he said from the other side of the door as he placed his arm in the free sleeve. "Thanks, again."

He exhaled a panicked breath and slowly replaced it with country air. "Nothing to worry about. I'm rich. Gorgeous wife. Great sex." He took another deep breath and repeated, "Nothing to worry about."

He descended the stone steps in his new silver tennis jacket.

Manor Hill was the smaller of the sister hills. Her driveway extended from the porch to the garage and ran down the hill's moderate incline. Howie saw the gardener, who quietly tended to rows of herbs.

"Good morning," Howie said with a wave in passing.

He expected to hear a "Hello" or "Good morning to you" in return, but was quickly disappointed. He glanced back to see if the gardener had responded at all.

The man wore a large straw hat that shadowed his face. He held an herb delicately in one gloved hand and a pair of scissors in the other. With a clean, violent snip, the herb was separated from its stem and placed into a wicker basket.

Behind the gardener and beneath the green copper roof of the covered garage, the chauffeur in black busied himself polishing Howie's new convertible.

The chauffeur stooped on one knee just behind the right front tire of the white Jaguar. He ran the towel along the whitewall in a seamless counterclockwise movement, staring right through Howie.

Howie shivered and quickly looked away.

When he reached the bottom of Manor Hill, he was faced with the decision to either walk to the large iron gate to check the mail— did they even have a mailbox, and was there a servant for that, too?—or trudge up the steeper of the sister hills, the aptly named Willow.

He chose to investigate whether or not he owned a mailbox when he heard the bleating of a sheep, or was it a goat? His attention turned to Willow Hill. Gazing up, he spied a black goat chewing a mouthful of grass beneath the large sallow tree.

While he ascended the hill, he became aware of a grassy ledge not so prominent when viewed from the driveway. It obscured the grazing goat as well as the tree's trunk. When he neared the top of the hill, he heard another bleat, but when he stood on the summit, he found himself alone beneath the sallow tree.

He spun clockwise to take in the panorama, which consisted of a fenced-in farm with cows, pigs, and chickens and a small run-off lake to receive their waste. After a section of trees, a larger, unpolluted lake stretched out for some distance, ending at the docks belonging to far-off neighbors. More trees, and at their foot, a small cemetery surrounded by an iron fence. Still more trees. The manor, garage, and herb garden.

Connecting the points were dirt trails sparsely covered with grass. The driveway leading to the high brick wall and iron gate, and beyond that, the lonely stretch of road lined with trees on either side that led to the busy highway, reminded him that the rest of the world was not much farther away.

But nowhere in the beautiful vision near or far was there a goat: black, bleating, grazing, or otherwise.

Chapter Five

Howie went to turn the knob when the front door swung open. Reggie, ever diligent to faithfully perform his duties, stepped back to allow Howie's entrance. When Howie noticed Reggie's eyes had focused on his jacket, he hurried from the room to find Elise.

Reggie lunged forward to remove the jacket, but with Howie's back turned, he felt but a slight brush of cold fingertips on his back. Howie shivered at the thought of Reggie's icy hands touching his bare flesh.

After passing through the kitchen, the bay room, dining room, living room, and a study, he found a yet-undiscovered room, where his bride sat in a hydraulic salon chair. The outer wall was nothing but windows, leaving little room for shadows. Behind Elise, a servant with perfectly parted, pitch-black hair and pencil-line mustache pulled a fitted bouffant wig over her head.

"Howard, this is Ozzy. He's our hair stylist," she said.

Howie didn't bother to face the expressionless man. If he was anything like the other servants, there was no need to fake any interest in interaction. Instead, Howie looked intently at the pink hair piece as if were a rabid rodent about to leap from her head for his throat.

"You don't approve?" his observant wife asked.

"It's not what I want to run my fingers through," Howie confessed.

"It's fine, Ozzy." She fluffed the wig and looked into the mirror held before her. "Howard, it's just for our night out on the town. It, like everything else, comes off."

Before his blushing face returned to its normal color, she had stood up and kissed him on the cheek. "Sit down, dear."

"Just a second," he said, unzipping the tennis jacket.

A familiar cold hand rested on his shoulder. He jerked and spun out of the jacket to find Reggie walking off with it to the foyer's coat rack.

Howie shook off the memory of the hand and sat in the salon chair as instructed. "Do I really need a haircut?"

Ozzy draped the nylon cape over his shoulders and snapped it closed around his neck. With a kick and a spin, Howie rose to eye-level with the lavender ascot jutting from the stylist's black vest.

"Ozzy isn't a barber," she corrected him. "He does not *cut* hair; he *styles* it."

Ozzy grabbed a bottle of spray and covered Howie's caramel crown in a light mist.

"But I just had it...*styled* a few weeks ago," said Howie.

Ozzy slid the scissors across the stainless steel table. The unnerving sound, like fingers dragging across a chalkboard, demanded Howie's attention, but just as quickly, the soothing siren of her voice regained it.

"No, you had it *cut*. Trust me, this is quite different," she said.

When the scissors snipped, Howie flinched. "Jeez, give me a warning, will ya?" he snapped.

Ozzy didn't alter his execution in the slightest. He combed and snipped without hesitation or regard for his host.

"It's best to remain still while Ozzy works. He's not used to your fidgeting and squirming about," she said.

Howie tried his best to stay still, but he found it near impossibe with Ozzy's indiscriminate snipping around the ears and his merciless jabbing at the eyes to *style* Howie's bangs.

"Did you make plans for tonight?" Howie asked, his voice jumping in pitch each time the scissors snipped.

"Yes, darling. We'll be going to an art show with some very influential people, and afterward, we'll have dinner," she answered.

"That sounds fancy."

"You shouldn't use words like *fancy*, Howard. It makes you sound small."

"Wonderful?" he asked, noticing the brown locks of hair piling in his lap. He blindly pulled at the cape's folds to shake off the hair and watched it fall to his feet.

"Much better."

Ozzy held a mirror behind Howie while both men faced the full-length mirror before them.

Not seeing much difference, Howie shrugged.

"Thank you, Ozzy. It's fine," she said.

Ozzy flicked the switch on a blow dryer.

"How was your walk?" she asked.

"It was fine," Howie answered. "I see we have goats."

"Beg pardon?" she spoke above the noise.

"I saw a goat under the tree. It was black," he said, nearly yelling.

"We don't have goats. We have chickens, pigs, and cows."

"No, I said *a* goat, as in one *single* goat."

Ozzy turned off the dryer and returned it to the table.

"Really, Howard, you kid about the silliest things," she said.

Using a small brush, Ozzy cleaned Howie's neck, then undid the cape. With a jerky motion, the hydraulic chair lowered and Howie stood up, brushing off the itchy stubble that peppered his clothing.

"I wasn't kidding," he said.

"Of course you weren't, darling. Now, Howard, if you'll go to our room, you'll find the outfit that Theo has picked out for you. It will be hanging on the wardrobe door."

"I can't dress myself?"

"Don't be silly, darling, of course you'll dress yourself; Theo isn't a pervert."

"I'm starting to miss the days when I was just a brick mason called Howie."

"Don't complain, dear. There are those much worse off who wish they had your petty hardships. Now be a doll and hurry back. Eddie and I will be waiting for you in the carport."

"Eddie?"

"The chauffeur."

"Of course. Eddie, the chauffeur," he repeated in a higher pitch, as if talking to a child on his way from the room.

When Elise heard him running up the stairs, she rebuked him. "A big man doesn't dash up the stairs like an anxious boy."

The beat of his steps decelerated. "You said to hurry," his voice echoed in the high-ceilinged foyer.

"Ozzy, collect his hair," she ordered.

Ozzy took a dustpan and broom from beside the stainless steel trash bin, stooped over, and swept Howie's tawny locks into the dustpan.

On the table stood an intricately carved silver box. Elise placed her fingers on the sides of the lid and pulled it back, revealing a black velvet-lined interior. Ozzie held the full dustpan to the box's edge and tipped it till the contents slid inside. Then, with a push of her finger, the silver lid snapped shut.

"Thank you, Ozzy. That will be all," she said.

He turned and left the room.

Chapter Six

In the weeks that followed, Howie found himself rubbing shoulders with artists, city planners, mayors, designers, and architects of renown. Elise was grooming him to be a true man of the world, one able to recognize a salad fork, carry himself in conversation, dress for success, and how to properly compliment—and even insult—his peers.

Every night the sex was always new and exciting; Elise never ceased to amaze him, and in this process, he surprised himself at how capable a lover he was becoming.

But something continued to gnaw at him.

Just like the formal ties he found himself tightening around his neck, this life of supposed finery and ease was slowly and surely choking the life out of him, restricting his breathing, his mobility. He felt boxed in, like a veal calf: fed, fattened, and tenderized into this thing that could be so easily led by the hand. And even if his intended destination rested far past the slaughter house to the high pedestal where only a golden calf could stand—for she in part idolized him—he was still an object, just one covered in flesh rather than gold. Still, for such a demanding person, she was completely irresistible.

Chapter Seven

Howie and Elise emerged from the revolving doors into the large foyer of Canning Hall. The room was abuzz with couples in formal evening dress, some chatting with other couples, others moving about the building's first and second floor. Howie witnessed its invigorating effect on Elise when he saw the corner of her mouth curl into a smile.

"You live for this stuff, don't you?" he asked, placing his hand at the small of her back.

She leaned into his chest while they walked. "I live for *you*, darling."

He pulled her closer. She placed a hand on his back and stomach, which protested with a growl. She snickered.

"For a five-star restaurant, I still have a five-star appetite," he joked. "They sell hot dogs and beer at this joint?"

"Don't be daft, darling. This isn't a football game."

"They do have bathrooms, right?"

"Of course," she said, stopping to locate them. She pointed to the left. "Over there."

"Good. I'm going to lose a glass of wine. Be right back," he said, and kissed her.

"While you're in the privy, I'll see if I can round up a program guide," she said.

"Sounds good," he said, then disappeared beyond the milling crowd.

She looked about the floor for an usher.

"Excuse me, ma'am," a masculine voice spoke.

She turned around to find a young man in an usher's uniform.

"Would you be needing a program guide?" he asked, pulling one from the top of the pile he held in his other hand and offered it to her.

"What marvelous timing, you have—" Her eyes ran down from his handsome face and quickly settled on his name tag. "—Bart. Thank you. I will take one." She smiled and accepted the program, which was printed on sturdy cardstock. "Thank you."

"You're welcome," he said, letting his eyes take her in.

Howie exited the bathroom, rubbing his hands together, then wiping them on his pants. He stooped down and took a sip from the water fountain, and when he stood and turned around, he nearly walked into a beautiful blonde.

"Lily?" he asked.

"Howie!" she squealed, and threw her arms around him.

Howie received her embrace, and only when old, fond memories began to work their way to the surface, did he pull away. They smiled at one another. When patrons entering and exiting the bathrooms in a steady stream express their disapproval at their blocking the path, Howie placed a hand on Lily's back. "Guess it's a little crowded here. We should probably move on," he said, and led her to the foyer. "Well, fancy meeting you in a fancy, er, wonderful place like this."

She looked about the expansive room with its domed-glass ceiling and clear view of the night sky. "It's not bad," she said, her eyes lowering to his. "What have you been up to since the wedding?"

"This and that. I don't get out much," he said, and looked around. "Are you here with Rich?"

"No."

"Are you two still an item?"

"It's nothing serious. We just go out from time to time."

"Okay. Well, look, anytime you two want to come up to the manor, you're more than welcome. Elise and I would love to have you over for dinner."

"'The manor.' What's it like saying `the manor'?"

He shrugged.

"I'm sorry. I know I'm a geek. I just can't believe your luck. What's it like having servants waiting on you hand and foot?" she asked.

"It takes some getting used to, to be honest."

"I bet. Massages, mannies, and peddies. I would get used to it *really* quick."

"Not with *their* hands, you wouldn't," he mumbled.

"What?"

"Let's just say freedom to do what you want when you want isn't a bad thing."

"Listen to you, acting like you're a prisoner."

Elise approached the two friends and stood between them. She leaned back so her body looked like a slash mark separating the two, and its language spoke just as much—that is to say, "Who is she and you're talking to her, why?" With her chin tucked into her throat, Elise eyed Lily from toe to head, then shifted her gaze to her husband.

"Honey, do you remember Lily, from the wedding? She was with Rich," he said.

"Not particularly," she said, and held out her hand limply for Lily to take, never moving her eyes from Howie.

"Before the wedding, we hadn't seen each other since high school," he said.

Lily began to fold the hand in hers, but Elise callously pulled it away. "I'm glad you've had plenty of time to catch up," said Elise, then shifted her attention to Lily. "Your husband is rich?"

Lily glanced at Howie when answering. "No. *Rich* was Howie's best man—at the wedding?"

Elise offered a disinterested humph and a "That so?" and an "I see," before returning her attention to her husband. "Howard, darling, we really should find our seats in the balcony before the show starts. You don't need to be wandering around trying to find your way in the dark. You could end up sitting beside who knows what."

"It was nice seeing you," said Lily, only offering Elise a quick glance before settling her eyes firmly on Howie.

"You, too," said Howie. "And don't forget about that invitation."

"Invitation?" said Elise, her golden-brown eyebrows arching high.

"Yes," said Howie and Lily at the same time. When they realized they answered simultaneously, they looked at each other and laughed, the way teenagers laugh when they know they're thinking the same secret thought.

"Yes," said Lily, and giggled with Howie again when they both heard the answer repeated. "Howie—"

"Howard," Elise corrected Lily.

"—invited me over for dinner," Lily finished, intentionally ignoring Elise's correction.

"Very well," said Elise. "I wouldn't want to disappoint you, so do give us a ring when the *two* of you plan to visit. I would hate to be a bad hostess."

"Oh, wait, Howie. Did you mean Rich and *me*, or just me?" Lily requested his clarification.

"*Howard* meant the two of you," Elise volunteered an answer.

"Okay," Lily said, and gave Howard the same awkward glance she found herself giving him each time Elise addressed her. "Oh, speaking of a *ring*, I suppose I'll need your phone number."

Lily removed her cell phone from her designer purse and began pressing keys to enter his name.

"Very well, it is—" Elise started to give her number when Howie interrupted.

"*My* number is 555-6677," he said.

"Great. I'll get with you soon, Howie," said Lily, then gave him a hug with her eyes closed. She held the kiss just long enough to feel Elise's burning stare before pulling herself away and returning the cell phone to her purse. "It was nice meeting you again, Elise."

Elise offered a cold half-smile. "I'm sure," she said, and linked Howie's arm with her own. "Now let's hurry before the lights go down."

While Lily walked away, she overheard Elise say, "Was that thing an old girlfriend?"

"Condescending bitch," Lily mumbled.

Chapter Eight

Elise held the strap of her tiny tangerine purse with both hands while Reggie gently removed her mink stole. "Howard, I'll be busy for a while, getting my beauty treatment," she said. "You go read a book or something."

"Sure. I'll keep myself busy. Did you plan on turning in when you're done?" he said.

"No, dear. I told you this morning what our plans were. Besides, Ricky won't be that long, will you?" she said, turning to the servant.

Ricky wore a black t-shirt and thigh-high shorts. A white sweatband crowned his clammy forehead, and a heavy towel hung over his left arm. While his curled, orange locks and thick, chevron mustache would typically lend themselves to a be-freckled complexion, every bit of his face was blindingly ivory white. He was the first servant Howie observed dressed in informal attire. Still, Ricky's answer was a mere wave of his right arm, signaling his mistress to proceed before him.

Howie watched the two walk together down the opposite hall and through the entertainment room, where the hardwood turned to carpet. On the far side of the room stood the doorway to the spa, where the floor changed again to marble tile. He heard their footsteps change in timbre as they crossed each.

Howie retired to the master bedroom for the evening. He stood before the full-length mirror, combing his hair to appear his best for what was sure to be another sexual marathon. When he ran the comb through his hair, he discovered there was now much less thanks to his earlier appointment with Ozzy.

A black blur passed behind him, and just as quickly passed into the bathroom. Howie spun about to see who it was, but there was nobody there. He wandered into the bathroom and found Phil in the corner. The stoic servant was filling a large, white sack with dirty laundry from the wicker hamper. When he was done, he turned around with the full sack dangling from one hand to find Howie standing just inside the room.

"I was wondering if you could make a bubble bath? For Elise, of course. Or, is *draw* the proper term? Yes, I'd like you to *draw* a bubble bath for Elise, alright?"

When Phil didn't answer, Howie reluctantly patted him on the shoulder. "Thanks, Phil. I appreciate it." Then he turned away. He'd only taken a few steps when he realized Phil was practically on his heels. The servant had matched him step for step, but dared not advance in the slightest movement toward his master, stopping abruptly as if he had an ON/OFF switch.

"I know Elise said you pretty much mind your own business, and I appreciate that, but if we ever do bother you, you know, keep you from getting a good night sleep or something, just let me know, all right?"

Phil didn't even blink.

"You know, 'cause I have a little something special planned for our evening, if you know what I mean. That's what the bubble bath is for. Set the mood, get things off to a good start, you know," Howie said, then offered a playful left hook to Phil's arm.

When Howie's hand connected, Phil's eyes slowly trailed down until they landed on the place of contact. Phil's lack of levity only encouraged Howie to try his resolve.

"Yes, me and Elise will be going at it pretty hard tonight," Howie started.

Phil's eyes gradually returned to face Howie.

"You're gonna hear screams, but don't worry, she won't be in any danger. I'm talking one hundred percent pleasure palace. The whole manor is gonna shake. Pictures and mirrors are gonna fall off the walls, and you'll have to put them all back. That gonna be a problem?"

Phil didn't crack a smile, or even twitch a single muscle. He stood face to face with Howie, unable to pass him. Howie sighed and stepped out of the way, letting Phil exit.

"No sense of humor," Howie mumbled as he reached for his toothbrush.

After he made himself presentable, he undressed and took a fresh bathrobe from the clothing rack on the wall. He took a seat on the bed and waited for Phil to return...and waited.

He opened the bedroom door and walked out into the hall and approached the railing. The sound of a running vacuum cleaner filled the foyer from floor to ceiling. Howie looked down to see Phil busy vacuuming the thick rug.

"You guys listen as good as you speak," said Howie, shaking his head.

He returned to the bathroom and prepared the bubble bath himself. With his arm submerged to the elbow, he gauged the temperature. When the tub had filled, he turned off the water.

He looked at his $500.00 wristwatch on the bathroom counter. The second hand ticked away endlessly. He went to the bedroom and placed the watch on the nightstand by his side of their plush bed and waited for Elise.

Chapter Nine

She stood on the threshold in a red satin nighty trimmed with black feathers, her back and the sole of her left foot resting against the door frame. She caught Howie in bed mid-yawn.

"Don't give out on me yet, tiger," she said.

He sat up against the brass railed headboard and finished his yawn. "Sorry," he said.

"No need to apologize. Perhaps it's better that you reserved your energy because I'm about to rock your world," she said, then blew on the collar of her nighty so that a single feather went floating in the air. It spun, caught in the cyclone of the ceiling fan, and flitted about the room.

"Before we get started, let me show you what I prepared for

you," he said with an eager, boyish smile.

"Do tell," she said, then skipped to him with an equally youthful demeanor.

He stepped out of bed and lifted her into his arms to carry her into the bathroom. Her head fell back and she giggled with closed eyes while he smothered her neck with kisses.

When she felt gravity take hold of her body, she turned her head and opened her eyes to see the white foamy waters about to engulf her. "No, Howie!" she screamed as her feet dipped into the bath.

He felt the painful pop his spine made when he stopped mid-motion. She apologized when she saw the grimace on his face.

"No, no, it's all right," he said, lowering her till her feet rested flat on the bathroom tile. He slowly and painfully straightened up.

"It's just that I dislike baths. *Really* dislike them."

"Obviously. You don't have to repeat yourself," he said, nursing his back with one hand.

"You've hurt yourself," she said, and reached out to touch his back.

He pulled away from her touch. "No, I'm all right. Just part of the job. All in the line of duty to make my master happy, just like her many other servants."

"Howard, you don't have to be spiteful."

"Who's being spiteful? I'm just following orders," he said. "If you don't want a bubble bath that I took all this time to make for you because none of the servants do a thing I ask, it's completely up to you. Your decision." He leaned against the wall with his arms over his head to stretch his back.

She sat on the edge of the tub. "Really, Howard, it was a lovely thought, but I'm a grown woman, not a toddler. And anyhow, you should know by now far more exciting things happen when we wind up in the shower."

She reached into the tub and pulled the stopper's beaded chain. Howie watched the level of white foam lower as the soapy water spiraled steadily down the drain.

"I'll see you in bed," he said, and left the bathroom.

As the last bubbles disappeared down the drain, she turned her head and sighed.

Chapter Ten

Howie awoke, a flash of light piercing his eyelids. He rolled over expecting to see Elise in a blissful sleep, but she wasn't there.

"Elise?" he called.

A flash of lightning. He waited, but the sound of thunder did not follow.

Maybe it was the unseasonable temperatures that brought about such late night storms, but heat lightning was usually distant, like a rainbow or a mirage, always a little farther beyond. He would have pondered such meteorological mysteries until sleep returned, but curiosity drew him out of bed. The cold floor permeated the soles of his feet and rose to his shins. The breeze from the ceiling fan chilled the rest of him. He made his way to the window, though it seemed more like he was being led on a leash by a hand holding the tether so loosely he only convinced himself he was free.

Outside, the full moon bathed the hillside in silver light. There, beneath the sallow tree, stood two slender figures in silhouette: one was a man, and the other was, without a doubt, Elise.

She presented something to the man. Moonlight gleamed along its edges to reveal a metal box. When she opened it, the man bowed his head to peer inside, and after a moment, he looked at her as a pearl-white smile shone across his face.

He raised his hands to her face, the she fell to her knees and embraced his waist.

Howie could not stand to watch any further. His shoulders caved, and he stumbled back to bed, trembling as he teetered back and forth from clench-fisted fury to utter heartache. He collapsed.

Chapter Eleven

"Howard? Howard, darling?" said Elise. She shook Howie by the shoulder and patted his cheek. "You fell out of bed."

His eyelids fluttered. He fought to keep them open as he tried to focus on her. "Why, Elise?" he mumbled.

"You slept too close to the edge. How should I know, dear?"

"No, Elise. Why?"

"Oh, my poor dear," she said and pulled his face into her bosom.

Chapter Twelve

As Howie's eyes slowly opened, he saw brilliant rays of light pulsating and shooting across the room. When his sight cleared, he found himself gazing into a round mirror. It gracefully crowned the regal head of the elderly doctor leaning over him.

"He'll be fine," said the doctor to Elise.

"What happened?" asked Howie, finally coherent, laying in his bed.

"You got up too quick. Faster than your blood pressure allowed, anyhow," said the doctor. "Did you have a bit too much to drink, perhaps?"

"He did have a few glasses of wine at dinner," she answered for him.

"Not that much," argued Howie.

"Good thing you have a designated driver, then," the doctor joked. "What's that fellow's name?"

"I'm sorry?" said Elise.

"Your driver," the doctor clarified.

"Eddie," answered Howie.

"Yes, Eddie," said the doctor.

"You remembered. Good," Elise praised him.

"Well, you just get some rest. Take it easy. No strenuous exercise for him," said the doctor, looking from Howie to Elise.

"I'll try not to keep him up too late," said Elise.

If Howie was too tired for anything, it was her sexual innuendos. He didn't flatter her with a blush.

The doctor closed the black leather bag on the floor and picked it up. "Call me if anything changes."

"Thank you, Doctor Medella. I will," she said.

His footsteps echoed down the hall, growing softer until a door closed.

"Howard, you gave me a fright," said Elise, seating herself beside her husband.

He smirked and looked away.

"Go ahead. Rest, darling," she said, and stroked his hair until he closed his eyes. Then she stood from the bed and left the room.

Chapter Thirteen

Elise sat at the bay room table, reading the morning newspaper. When Howie stepped into the room, he noticed both places had been set at the table.

"Howard. You're up," she said, peering over the newspaper.

He wore blue jeans and a gray sweater jacket. He complimented the outfit with a black leather belt, blue scarf, and silver-rimmed shades.

"And dressed, too. Going somewhere?" she asked.

"I couldn't stay in bed all day," he said, taking the spare piece of buttered toast from Elise's plate.

Her eyes followed the toast from her plate to his mouth. He ignored her expression of disapproval.

"How are you feeling?" she asked.

"Like I need to go for a ride. Where are the keys to the Jag?" he said with a full mouth.

"You don't need to be driving in your condition.

"I don't have a condition."

"All the same, I would rest easier knowing Eddie is behind the wheel."

"I'm fine. The doc says I'm fine. What's there to worry about?" he asked and poured a glass of fresh milk from the cold stainless steel pitcher.

"Considering your recent episode, I think it's in your best interest to have someone keep an eye on you."

He took several swallows of milk. "I'm not convinced I had an episode."

"Ridiculous, Howard. Besides, as a man of the world, you need to always put your best foot forward. That's what Eddie is for."

He pulled his shades down to the tip of his nose. "I'd much rather put *my* foot down. On the pedal. Myself. Keys?" he said, and held out his hand.

She gazed at his open palm, then into his eyes. She flipped a page and returned to her newspaper. "There'll be no further discussion. Eddie is taking you, and that's final. When you're done with your excursion, he'll be waiting to bring you home."

Howie's fist snapped shut like a bear trap. His jaws clenched, and his breathing grew louder. He raised his shades and exited the room with intentionally heavy steps.

"Don't stomp, Howard. You sound like a lumbering elephant,"

she said.

Somewhere in the house, a door slammed, evoking a flinch from Elise. She shook her head. "Nothing but an overgrown boy," she muttered.

She placed the newspaper on the table and approached a wall-mounted pager with several buttons. She pressed one labeled GARAGE.

Howie trotted down the small wooden steps into the covered garage, where Eddie stood at full attention by the passenger side door of the Jaguar.

"How's it going, Eddie?" asked Howie, expecting no answer.

Eddie opened the door.

"Oh, you want to ride along?" asked Howie.

Eddie stood by the door, his hand still on the handle.

"Well, go ahead. Get in, I'll drive," said Howie, but Eddie stood still.

Howie looked at the empty passenger seat, then at Eddie. He walked past Eddie and ran his hand along the curved hood of the car. "Wow, you got this thing looking great," he said.

Howie glanced at the black limo and orange Corvette parked behind the Jaguar. He approached the shiny Corvette and ran his hand along its hood, then examined his fingertips.

"Can't say the same about the 'vette. When's the last time you washed it?" he asked.

He watched Eddie for a reaction, hoping the ploy would work. Instead, Eddie walked to the opposite side of the Jaguar and opened the door.

"Thanks, Eddie," Howie said, and rushed to the driver side to squeeze in, but Eddie seated himself and pulled the seat belt strap over his shoulders.

"You know, I *can* drive. Wouldn't you like the afternoon off? And if not, you can always detail Elise's 'vette," he suggested.

Eddie turned the key in the ignition, and the car started.

"There's no reasoning with you guys, is there?" said Howie.

He watched the black-gloved hands embrace the steering wheel. His head dropped in defeat. He circled the car and sat in the passenger's seat. When he pulled the door shut, Eddie put the Jaguar in gear and pulled out of the shaded garage into the sunny day.

As they drove down the red brick road to the iron gate, Howie retrieved his cell phone from his pocket and began mashing keys. After a moment a tone sounded. He read the message.

LILY: Since when did you start texting?

He responded. "When I became a prisoner in my own car."

LILY: ???

"Explain over lunch. Be there soon."

LILY: K. C U there.

Eddie took a remote control from the dash, and with the press of a button, the iron gate swung upon, allowing the car to leave the estate.

Chapter Fourteen

As the foyer door closed behind Howie, the noise of the busy street was cut off, replaced with the sound of conversation and clanking dishes. He saw her seated at the far end of a small table by the window. She gazed outside like a daydreaming child on a school bus.

"Name, sir?" the host asked.

"I'm with the young lady," said Howie, pointing at Lily.

"Very good," the host said, taking a menu from a wall-mounted holder. "Right this way, please."

Howie followed him to the table, set with glasses of water and silverware atop linen napkins. Lily turned away from her imagined kingdom and stood to offer Howie a warm hug, which he gratefully received.

The embrace was so affirming that Howie hated for it to end. He stood there with closed eyes, absorbing as much of her as he could.

The host discreetly dropped the menu on the table. "You two enjoy," he said, then returned to his foyer podium.

"Oh, it's been too long," said Lily, likewise savoring the moment.

Howie sighed and forced himself to pull away after a final caress of her back. The two stood at arms' length, their hands still cradling the other's back.

"Look at you," she said, her head tilted and eyes sparkling.

"Look at me? Look at you," he said.

"Oh, stop," she said, her cheeks coloring.

"No, really. You look great."

She looked toward the window.

As he followed her gaze, he remembered he was short on time. "Shall we?" he asked.

"Yes," she answered with a smile.

He involuntarily reached to pull her chair out for her, but she had already begun to sit. "Oh," he said, his hand nervously retreating to massage his neck before pulling his own chair from under the table and taking a seat.

She smiled. "Were you going to pull my chair out for me?"

"It's habit," he said, staring down at the table, his face red with embarrassment.

"That's sweet. I see your wife has trained you well."

He smirked and nodded, his eyes still on the table. "Yeah, about that," he quipped before their waiter arrived.

"Have you made your decision?" asked the young man in formal attire.

"Yes. I'll have the arugula salad and your soup of the day," said Lily. "Oh, and a glass of Pinot Noir."

"Very good, Madam. And for you, Sir?" the waiter asked Howie.

"My apologies. I haven't looked at the menu yet. Do you have Beef Bourguignon?" Howie asked.

"We do. An excellent choice, by the way, Sir," the waiter said, writing the order down.

"Oh, and could you make the lady's Pinot Noir a bottle of Volnay?" asked Howie.

"Certainly, Sir. Very good," said the waiter with a bow of his head. He collected the menus, then turned and took their orders to the kitchen.

Lily stared at Howie with her mouth open. She blinked and shook her head.

"I hope that wasn't too forward," he said.

She sighed. "Not at all. I'm actually impressed."

"Where were we?"

She closed her eyes a moment to recollect. "So. 'Prisoner in your own car'?" she asked.

"Yes. The warden is a charming fellow, like the rest of them," he answered with no attempt to hide his sarcasm.

"There you go again, making them sound like prison guards."

"Trust me, Lily. You can't take two steps without one of them stomping on your heels and breathing down your neck."

"You know what they say if you're rich and unhappy?"

"What's that?"

"You're doing it wrong."

"Maybe so. But if you don't mind, can we talk about something else besides my new-found wealth?"

She slouched forward and clasped her hands, her eyes full of pity. "You know, when you haven't seen someone in twenty years, you *are* supposed to talk about new-found wealth. And love," she said, making it a point of looking at the naked ring finger on her left hand as she circled the rim of the glass with her index finger. She shifted her focus to his face and her voice softened. "Or love lost."

"We all grow up. I'm sure you're not working at that ice cream store anymore."

"You remember that?"

"I never forgot. Didn't you ever wonder why I took so long to choose the same old flavor?"

"I assumed you were indecisive."

His eyes locked with hers momentarily. "I've always known what I wanted."

She sat up straight, and faced the window again. "But you settled for love and money instead?"

He cleared his throat. "It's more demanding than you think."

"Which?" she asked. "Love or money?"

He was contemplating an answer when the waiter arrived with the bottle of Volnay and two glasses. After uncorking the bottle and filling the glasses, he left them to their conversation.

Lily took a small swallow. "Very nice," she said.

"I'm glad you like it," he said. He took a sip and savored the taste before swallowing.

"It's a good thing you have a chauffeur. I don't think you'll be in any position to drive if we finish this."

He laughed. "And you?"

"I walked here from the office. I'll take a cab."

"Good. Now where were we?" he asked.

"Oh yes, ice cream," she said. "I have indeed left the frozen dairy industry behind for better things, namely underwriting events such as The Music Box ballet for one of the top three law firms in the city."

"Now I'm impressed."

"One of the perks includes free passes to shows. Unfortunately, that includes a lot of ballet, which hasn't been my thing since I retired my leotard when I was six."

He smiled. "I wouldn't call our bumping into one another unfortunate."

She stared at his lips. "No. I wouldn't either," she said, returning the smile.

After more small talk, the waiter arrived with their meals and placed them before his guests. "Bon appetit," he said and took his leave.

Between bites and more wine, they fell into more relaxed conversation, and after a half an hour, the bottle stood nearly empty.

The waiter arrived and placed the black checkbook on the table. "Whenever you are ready," he said, then turned away to attend to other diners.

Lily twirled her wrist, the wine sloshing against the rim of the glass she held. She set it down. "So," she said, mischief in her eyes. "How's the sex?"

He choked on the wine as his eyes went wide. He was quick to recover, then said, "Wow. You just went there."

"You knew I would. I just want to make sure you're—you know—satisfied."

He stared at his own ring finger. The gold band suddenly seemed dull in the dim light, and it didn't sparkle half as much as Lily's honest eyes. He swallowed and raised his eyes. "Why wouldn't I be?"

"She seems a little on the cold side to me. But maybe you like your women like you like your ice cream."

He laughed. "She's no ice cream cone."

"So, it's okay? Mediocre? Mind-blowing?"

"You won't stop, will you?"

She smiled at him devilishly. "No."

"Fine. All you need to know is that what they say about older women is true."

"What's that?"

"They know how to please a man."

"Well, don't go counting us spring chickens out just yet. We still have a few tricks up our sleeves," she said with that devilish smile.

"Speaking of able-bodied spring chickens, why are you waiting to settle down?"

"That's just it. I don't want to settle for settling down. I want some-one with a future, somebody with aspirations. Somebody going places."

"You know, I'm now in Elise's circle of friends. I've met a few high-rollers. Some eligible bachelors, even."

"Sorry, Howie, I'm not looking for a sugar daddy. Older men can't please me, and money is only a temporary substitute for bad sex."

He laughed and placed his hands on the table.

"Who knows," she continued. "Maybe when I'm Elise's age I'll find someone like you." She reached across the table and took his right hand in hers.

He placed his left hand over theirs and smiled. "I don't doubt someone like you can do much better than me," he said.

She looked into his eyes. "Why do you keep downing yourself? Whether you know it or not, you're a real keeper, Howie."

The way she said his name. He loved it. He sighed.

"What?" she asked.

He smiled, and his eyes trailed away.

"Hey, you," she said, pulling his hand.

He stared at the empty street. "I think Elise is having an affair."

Her shoulders dropped.

He faced her. "I saw her with one of the servants last night."

"Are you sure?" she asked, her eyes filled with pity.

"Yeah."

"What are you going to do?"

"What should I do? I'm rich. We have great sex, and I'm moving up in the world. I have no worries."

"But—"

"Isn't that all that matters, Lily?"

She looked at her plate.

A rap came on the window. The startled friends turned toward the window to find Eddie standing there, looking down at their joined hands.

Howie jerked his hands away. Eddie was now staring at him with that deer-in-the-headlights gaze he had grown accustomed to from all his wait staff.

He tore his attention away from the chauffeur and looked down at his watch. With a sigh, he said, "Looks like I lost track of time."

Eddie knocked again.

"Alright. I'm coming!" said Howie.

He opened the book and looked at the check.

"I wanted to—" Lily began.

"It's my treat," said Howie. "Besides, if I'm going to spend my wealth on anything, I would prefer to spend it on my friends. *Real* friends."

He retrieved two hundred-dollar bills from his wallet and placed them inside the book and closed it. "I hate to rush, but it looks like I better get going before he wears a hole in the glass," he said.

"I understand."

He stood. "I enjoyed catching up."

"Me, too."

She got up from her chair, pulled the black leather purse strap over her bare shoulder and gave him a brief hug. "Call me," she said.

"I will. Soon," said Howie.

All the while Eddie stood behind the glass rapping, rapping away, like a strange, curious creature in an aquarium; or maybe the annoying boy on the outside of one who ignores the sign that plainly states, "Do not tap on the glass." He didn't stop until Howie and Lily left the table.

Outside, Howie found Eddie standing by the limo, the rear passenger side door already open.

"What happened to the Jag?" he asked Eddie in vain.

Elise's voice emanated from the interior of the limo. "Tell me, are you in the habit of fanning old flames?"

"What?" Howie asked.

"Come now. Sit inside. We haven't all day," she ordered from the back seat.

He climbed in beside her, then Eddie shut the door.

"Do I have to repeat myself?" she said once they had pulled away from the curb.

"Lily is a friend," said Howie.

"For her sake, she best be. I can be extremely jealous, Howard."

"Maybe I can, too."

"Just what do you mean by that, exactly?"

"What old flames have *you* been fanning?"

"I don't like your tone of voice."

"And I don't like your midnight rendezvous with the gardener, the plumber, or whichever dumb waiter I saw you with."

"Don't insult the help. You wouldn't want to be on *their* bad side, either. And since you brought it up, exactly when was it you *thought* you saw me with a servant?"

"Last night. By the willow tree, if that jogs your memory."

"You must have been dreaming. Or perhaps you hallucinated during your spell."

"I know what I saw," he said, but a nagging thought gnawed at him. How had he been able to see everything that took place atop Willow Hill so plainly and from such distance--as if he were floating somewhere between the window and the hill, and that wasn't possible. "At least I'm truthful about who I visit."

The conversation ended on that sour note. Soon the car turned down the private road that led to Sallow Manor. She closed her eyes and massaged her left temple. Howie could hear her breathing.

He took a deep breath himself and thought about the words he wanted to say but refrained. When the car came to the open gate, Howie spoke up. "Let me out."

"Beg pardon?" said Elise.

He opened the car door. "I said, let me out."

"Have you gone mad?"

"Tell him to stop."

"Tell him yourself."

"Stop kidding, Elise. You know they don't listen to a word I say."

"Eddie, stop the car," she said.

The chauffeur's hollow eyes met hers in the rear view mirror. When the car came to a complete stop at the foot of the sister hills, Howie stepped out.

"Howard, what are you doing?" she asked.

"I need a moment alone."

"Don't be ridiculous, dear. Get back in the car."

"I *said*, I *need* a moment!"

The car idled on the driveway. Elise stared at Howie through the open car door, her hands atop the purse in her lap. "Would you mind—" she asked, but Howie was already walking away. She leaned over and pulled the car door shut. "Drive, Eddie," she grumbled.

When the limousine's purring engine faded in the distance, Howie heard the bleating of a goat. He peered up the hill and saw the black beast beneath the sallow tree. He couldn't be sure if it was the same one he saw before, but he was certain his eyes weren't playing tricks on him.

He hurried up the steep grade, moving quietly to avoid startling the goat. The bleating of the animal grew louder.

"*No, Howard. We don't have any goats,*" he mumbled under his breath. "That sure as hell isn't a pig."

When he neared the top of the hill, he found himself on his knees clutching handfuls of grass and staring at a pair of Italian leather shoes. He gazed up to see which of the servants stood before him, but he only saw a figure backlit by the afternoon sun.

Staring at the rays that seemed to emanate from the man's face, an image flashed in his mind from the dream he had weeks before: gargoyles perched atop his monolithic masterpiece turning in unison to behold the rising sun, though at present the words "Morning Star" came to him. Howie stood and shielded his eyes from the sun with a hand. "So which of the useless servants are you?"

"I wouldn't exactly call myself useless." The man spoke in the accent of a proper Southern Gentleman.

When Howie lowered his hand, the stranger's features became clear. The suit he wore was sleek and crisp, not at all like the uniforms the waitstaff wore. But much like everyone in Elise's world, he was Caucasian, and the first to show the barest hint of color, indicating that he saw the sun on occasion. The handsome man was further distinguished by dark gray hair and sharply chiseled bones that graced both cheek and jaw.

"I don't believe it. Someone who speaks," said Howie.

"Among other talents. Are you impressed?" the man asked.

Howie wasn't. "You're the only man around here not doing the Marceau Marceau impersonation."

"Nicholas," said the man, offering a hand.

Howie didn't take it. "Are you the one I saw Elise with last night?"

Nicholas' friendly smile faded as he lowered his hand. "Mayhaps. Elise and I do meet from time to time to discuss certain—*business* matters."

"That's what you call it?"

"Whatever you think you saw was just that. Business."

"Then I don't appreciate you having any business with her."

"*Howie*, is it?"

For once, Howie corrected someone. "Howard, *Nick*."

Nicholas tilted his head and smirked. "Now, correct me if I'm wrong, but I'm sure you have an associate or two outside of your marital relations?"

"If you mean a lover, no, I don't."

"Are you sure? Because Elise has her doubts. Recently mentioned someone named Lily," Nicholas said with a twirl of his finger.

"Lily is a friend."

"As am I."

"No. I saw what you two did. I would never do that with Lily."

Nicholas' chest shook with barely contained laughter. "Not even under the right conditions?"

"I said she's just a friend."

"Yes, I heard. A friend, you said. Now, how was it Elise put it?" His eyes wandered again, this time in recollection. "`She's younger, more attractive, and practically exuding sex through every pore.' Does that sound about right?"

Howie held his peace.

Nicholas smiled far too wide. "Don't worry, I understand. Everybody needs a ear to listen; a shoulder to cry on. Don't you think?" he said, reaching for Howie's shoulder.

Howie pulled away and wagged a finger at his adversary. "You're about two seconds away from having your ass handed to you on a platter."

Nicholas raised a hand, palm forward. "Howard, you misunderstand. What you witnessed between Elise and me was merely a transaction. She gave me something, and to show my gratitude, I gave her something in return."

"She was the only one giving anything from what I saw."

"I doubt your eyes are that good."

"My imagination works perfectly fine."

"Mayhaps it's a bit overactive. Would you care to see what she gave me?"

"No."

Nicholas reached inside his jacket and produced a silver box. With the ornate curio resting in his left hand, he opened the lid with his right.

"Take a gander," he said, glancing down at the box.

Howie leaned forward to have a glimpse. "What is that?" he asked.

"You don't know?"

"It's hair," said Howie, staring at the brown locks.

"*Your* hair. From a recent appointment with your barber, no doubt."

"Why do you have my hair?"

"Like I said before, it's just business," Nicholas said and snapped the lid shut before returning it to his jacket pocket.

"Am I under some kind of investigation?"

"It ain't no evidence; just an offering—in exchange for the power to control you."

"I don't see how having my hair is necessary. Elise seems to be doing a fine job of it."

"You don't believe in magic?"

"Like voodoo?"

"Something like that, yes. The point is, Elise wants control, Howard. Complete control. You see, she ain't never wanted a husband. She wants a house pet. And that's exactly what you are. Like a cat or dog. But you're not a cat," he said, wagging a finger. "At least a cat has a sense of pride and independence." He studied Howie closely. "No, Howard. You know what you are? You're a dog. A loyal lapdog.

Ever obedient at her beck and call."

"And you're the witch doctor?"

"And more. Have a seat," said Nicholas, motioning toward a small wrought iron table and chairs.

Howie scanned the hilltop, confused and wondering where the table and chairs had come from. "Where did—"

Nicholas sat. "Iced tea?" he offered, pouring himself a glass from a full pitcher. The clinking ice cubes were aglow with sunlight. He took a sip. "Ah. Best in the South. Would you care for a glass?"

With a firm grip on its barred back, Howie tested the chair to ensure it was solid before sitting opposite his host. "Sure. I'll take one."

"You see, Howard—" Nicholas said, slowly filling the glass. "—I delight in offering my services, but I'm not too much a stickler when it comes to principle. I offer my services to the highest bidder. Elise has placed her continuing loyalty on the table in exchange for eternal youth—relatively speaking of course—and control of your mortal soul. Now, as far as I can tell, you're more than content with your lot, but should you desire to raise the stakes, now would be the opportune moment."

He placed the pitcher on the table and handed the glass to Howie. "Hope you like that."

"You're kidding, right?" said Howie.

Nicholas leaned over the table and looked into Howie's eyes. "Howard, don't you want to be the greatest architect of the twenty-first century?"

Howie watched beading sweat run down the side of the tall glass before him. He stroked the cool glass with a finger, leaving a mist-free path behind it. "Ever since I was a boy, from the time I went to my first Mass at the Gothic basilica of St. Mary's, then my first field trip to the monuments and memorials in DC, to my first funeral—seeing my grandfather entombed in the marble mausoleum at Endless Rest Cemetery. From the cradle to man's highest achievement, to the grave, my life has been built around architecture, though I suppose the opposite could be said: architecture has been built around my life.

"I just knew I wanted to be the man who made those buildings what they were. I wanted to design the colossal columns reaching clear into space, the palisades, the great porches and giant stairs, the balconies, and the gargoyles perched way up high. Sometimes I wonder if it's just a fleeting fantasy."

"As they say, anything is possible," Nicholas said, and as he took a sip from his glass, he noticed Howie's. "You haven't touched your tea."

Howie raised the glass and took a long sip. He savored the sweetness of the Southern brew before answering. "It's so sweet. Elise would kill me."

Nicholas leaned back in his chair and crossed his legs. "Sometimes a man just needs to let loose. Don't you think?"

"If I let loose anymore, I might find myself on a very tight leash. Or in the doghouse."

"You know, Howie, life was meant to be sweet. I don't mean that whole 'when life gives you lemons' line. If some bitter person or event makes you and your life anything less than perfection, it's time to sweeten things up—like this iced tea."

"Drown my sorrows in iced tea, eh?"

"Exactly. *Drown* your sorrows. Drown whatever is keeping you down."

Howie laughed and twirled the cup. "Make that bitch an island and stand on top of it."

The ice cubes spun in a mesmerizing whirlpool.

"Yes, Howie," Nicholas smiled. "Drown that bitch."

Howie laughed so hard his sides hurt, and Nicholas guffawed right along. Howie doubled over in pain from laughter. Nicholas slapped his back.

Howie squeezed his tearing eyes tight and fought to catch his breath between bellows of laughter. He reached over to embrace Nicholas' arm. It was coarse and jagged, like—

Howie opened his eyes and found himself leaning against the sallow tree on the unfurnished, grassy hilltop. The gentle breeze blew the tall grass in waves. A bleat sounded in the distance. Howie ran to the edge of the hill and looked down. A black goat wandered down a dirt trail toward the iron-gated cemetery.

Sweat ran down Howie's forehead, into his eyes. He thought of the glass of iced tea he was sure he had held and even drank from. He took the same dirt trail the goat used and found it far less steep. In the distance he saw the goat, still headed toward the cemetery. When Howie reached the bottom, he rounded it to the manor.

He scaled the stairs in a dizzying fever, and with each labored step, the front entrance appeared to rock side to side as if the manor's foundation were afloat on a raging sea. He reached for the elusive door handle, but it dodged him left and right. After several attempts, he closed his eyes in frustration, and the handle found his palm.

He entered the foyer, where he heard Elise's voice echo from a distant room. The closer he came, the clearer his mind; the cooler his flesh. Manny passed him in the entertainment room. A grand piano stood to his left and before him a coffee table, and behind it laid Elise on a Victorian chaise lounge.

"Where's he headed?" Howie asked.

"Oh, Howard. Do be quiet, dear. I have a splitting migraine," she spoke softly, her eyes closed and the back of her wrist resting on her forehead.

"I'm sorry. I just—"

"He's on his way to prepare a kettle of tea for me. Now please, let me rest," she moaned.

"Yes, dear," he whispered, listening to Manny's slow steps echo through the hall. "I'll let you rest."

He left the room, and as quietly as he could, stepped up his pace.

He hurried past Manny. "Coming through, Man."

Howie ran into the kitchen and straight to the pantry door. He slung the door open and stepped inside, pulling the door shut behind him, When he turned around, he found the pantry to be larger than expected. He glanced around. There were boxes of dried fruits, baking soda, bags of flour, sugar, rice, beans, and finally, the teas, just as Elise described them—all labeled by ingredient and use in quart-sized bottles.

He read the handwritten labels, mumbling aloud, "Favor, Healing, Protection, Sleep."

He took the bottle and exited the pantry. He found the kettle among the pots and pans, all hanging from stainless steel hooks. He pulled the top off the kettle, then opened the bottle. He skimmed through the directions, mumbling aloud. "For...sleep drink one to two...before bedtime. One teaspoon per cup...Boil...steep...10 minutes...maximum effect."

He heard Manny's steps getting louder.

He rifled through cabinet drawers in search of a measuring cup. "Forget it!" he growled and poured at least a cup's worth of tea into the kettle.

A moan drew his attention. He turned to see Manny standing in the kitchen entrance.

"Here you go, Man," said Howie. "I got you started. See?"

Manny approached the table and picked up the kettle. He stared inside without blinking. He turned to Howie and, without looking away, placed the top on the kettle.

It wasn't quite a smile, but Manny opened his mouth and bared his teeth, none of them touching. It looked more like an expression of pain. He wore it even when he turned and walked with the kettle to the stove.

Howie left the kitchen and made his way up the foyer stairs to the master bedroom. He went into the bathroom and pulled the door shut.

Chapter Fifteen

She lay unconscious on the chaise lounge. The hand that had rested on her forehead now dangled over the side of the lounge. The kettle had been set down on a ceramic coaster on the coffee table, and on a smaller coaster rested the cup. He peered inside the cup to find half a swallow remained.

He stared at her face and whispered her name. He waited for a response. "Elise," he said a second time. Then he performed a third test: he placed his hand on her shoulder and shook her gently.

Content that she was out, he placed his arms beneath her, scooped her up from the chaise lounge, and carried her to the foot of the stairs. When he placed his right foot on the first step, she began to stir. With a soft grunt, she threw an arm over his shoulder. He stood still until settled down again, then continued up the stairs.

Having jogged up and down the stairs so often, he had never noticed the persistent stare of the painted men that lined the wall to his left. Their eyes followed him with each step, gazing at him, or maybe inside him, at the dark intentions that now motivated him, and yet, he wasn't sure if their expressions signified approval or damnation.

He reached the landing and crossed the walkway to the master bedroom. He pushed the door open with his foot and laid her on the plush, purple blankets of their bed. He walked softly to the bedroom door and locked it, then returned to the bed, where he took Elise in his arms and carried her into the bathroom.

He looked back at the open door. He wanted to lock it, but there was no place to lay Elise except the full bathtub.

"Elise," he whispered in her ear.

Her breast gently rose and fell, but she did not wake.

"Elise," he said, his voice cracking. He shook her softly. "Elise, honey. Wake up."

A tear ran down his cheek, joining the perspiration from his burden and the steamy room.

He lowered her to the tub, then gently eased her into it. The crushing wave of guilt crashed over him, bringing him to tears and to his knees. He buried his face into his arms atop the rim of the tub to sob, then sobs turned into laughter, and when laughter subsided, he turned his attention to the criminal task at hand.

The image in his mind moments before was of her submerged beneath the rushing water's surface, eyes wide open in a death stare.

Instead, he found her floating atop, eyes still closed. "What?"

He placed both hands on her chest and pushed down, but he was met with resistance. Instead of sinking to the bottom of the tub, she glided across the surface of the water until she bumped into the far wall. It was as though the water was rejecting her.

With furrowed brow, he pushed again, harder, but she just floated back toward him.

"How are you doing that?" he said.

He reached into the tub and filled his palm with water, which he poured over her face.

Her face twitched side to side as if her nose had been tickled by a feather. He tried again to push her below the surface, but she continued to hover over it. He reached for the faucet and turned both handles, releasing a torrent of water over her head.

With an angry scowl, he placed his hands around her throat and squeezed. Her face turned pink, then red. He squeezed harder. Her eyes shot open.

Chapter Sixteen

Elise couldn't understand why Howie's hands were so tightly wrapped around her throat, why his face was burning a fiery red and the vein in his temple throbbing, pounding—or why he was making such a dedicated attempt to force her beneath the gushing tap into the flooding tub.

Water sloshed over her face, in and out of her ears, removing sound one moment, allowing it the next—the sole sound being a constant maniacal note stuck somewhere in Howie's throat. It would be a sort of menacing growl if his throat tightened, closed just a fraction further, but alas, the murderous musical pitch refused to succumb to its lower nature.

Perhaps it was a result of too much refinement. Napkin, salad fork, dinner fork, dessert fork, service plate with soup bowl, dinner knife, teaspoon, soup spoon, from left to right, and above all, *no growling*.

After months of molding, shaping, and sculpting him into the perfect gentleman, he had collapsed under the weight of her heavy hands into this slobbering murderer. All her forced finery, her exacting etiquette, had melted away like a cheap glaze, revealing the misshapen half-baked vessel beneath.

The water sloshed over the tub's ceramic siding onto the marble floor. What a mess he was making. She stared at him queerly and spit a mouthful of water out as delicately as possible, even when he pushed her beneath the faucet again. She refused to fall into a fit of hysteria simply because he was attempting to murder her.

"Drown, bitch! Drown and let me live my life!"

Her brow furrowed and she huffed. Her neck became rigid; her head unmovable, unsinkable. First, he straightened one leg, then the other, and leaned all his weight into his forearms. When she saw the childish frustration in his raging, purple face, she couldn't help but burst into a wicked laughter that smashed his remaining resolve. The perfect crime and its flimsy walls fell like a house of cards, leaving his psyche completely exposed in all its undeniable humiliation.

His shoulders sagged and the white-knuckled fingers over her throat grew limp. His hands turned pink with the circulating blood. He stood up and stepped back until he hit the bathroom counter.

"Oh my darling, you really are a fool," she purred, stepping out of the tub. She reached back and turned off the water.

"What are you?" he dared to ask.

"You haven't figured it out? My knowledge of herbs and love of nature? The ancient religion I never found time to discuss? My dread of water? My midnight rendezvous with a mysterious man?"

"You m-mean Nicholas?"

"So you've met him."

He nodded fearfully.

"My ignorant school boy, have you never read of the various methods to expose or dispose of a witch? We're not one with nature for no reason. We and water have an understanding—we would never betray one another willingly. That's why the Puritans bound us with cords to heavy, wooden beams before throwing us into the water."

"A witch?" he asked incredulously.

She reached for a thick towel labeled HERS hanging from the mounted rod beside the tub. Beside it hung a robe labeled HERS, and beside them, a matching set labeled HIS. She stood and wrapped the large towel around her wet body.

With a glance back at the full tub of water, she said, "No offense taken, old friend."

The water bubbled its response before she pulled the drain plug.

"Now, to take care of you," she said, facing Howie. "Reggie!" she called out.

Howie turned and pulled the bathroom door shut and locked it.

"Fool. The servant *does* have keys," she said.

Howie looked about the counter top for anything to defend himself with. He spied his tweezers on a small hand towel, next to his nail clippers and trimming scissors. He heard the bedroom door swing open and heavy footsteps approach.

The bathroom door handle turned halfway. Howie heard the jangling of keys. He took the pair of scissors in his left hand and gripped the door handle with his right. The handle began to turn. He prevented it. A second attempt was made; the door cracked open. Howie dropped the scissors and used both hands to pull it shut.

A moan came from behind the door. A third attempt. The door didn't budge. Howie locked it again.

"It's only a matter of time," said Elise, amused at his struggle.

"Shut up!" shouted Howie.

Another moan.

"You shut up, too!" Howie yelled at the unseen servant.

Something slammed into the door, bowing it from the opposite side, Howie's shoulders flinched.

Elise laughed. "Still the little man you were when I met you. Pull yourself together. On second thought, why bother, since my suitors will soon tear you apart?"

Howie's expression was absolutely pitiful. Every muscle in his face went instantly limp. He looked around the bathroom again, this time for something to shield himself with.

To his right sat a plush velvet-cushioned chair with a high brass back. He took the chair and wedged it beneath the door handle.

"Is that the best you can do?" Elise teased him.

A cold, gray hand punched through the bathroom door and fumbled for the handle. Half-foot long splinters lined the hole the suited arm reached through.

Howie frantically scanned the counter again, then the floor until he located the pair of scissors. Gripping the makeshift weapon, he swung around and dug them into the servant's forearm.

The twin blades emerged from his flesh and muscle with a gleam of light, releasing a viscous flow of writhing maggots. They seeped out of the wound and plopped onto the floor like spoonfuls of raw cookie dough.

The gray hand took hold of the door handle and turned the lock, disregarding its injury. Despite Howie's best attempt, the chair merely slid aside with a squeal, and the door swung open.

Reggie eyed his mistress from head to toe for any sign of harm.

"Stop him, Reggie," she ordered. "He tried to kill me."

The servant turned to his former master with the first look of determination Howie had seen in his hollow eyes since coming to the estate. Reggie took the chair from behind the door and tossed it aside to squeeze his body through the doorway.

As the servant reached for his master, Howie shoved the door back toward him. Through the splintered hole in the door, Howie watched Reggie fall straight back, down to the floor without a single attempt to stop his fall or cushion the impact. His head hit the floor with a loud crack, like a cue ball breaking a rack of billiard balls.

Howie hesitated, waiting to see if Reggie got up. Sure he was dead, Howie pulled the door open, stepped over the corpse, and started toward the stairs. A moment later, the dead servant blinked. Reggie sat up, a squirming puddle of maggots on the floor where his broken head had rested, then struggled to get to his feet. Once he was up, proceeded to follow his mistress' order.

Howie made it to the end of the walkway when he saw the line of fearsome uniformed corpses ascending the stair. With his eyes fixed on the approaching threat, he watched the servants move like an animated figure in a zoetrope.

All hope of escape crumbled; his dreams of collapsing like a building under demolition; the master architect undone. Reggie's cold hands gripped Howie's shoulders. He didn't flinch. There was no need to resist the inevitable. He fell to his knees.

Elise stepped from the bedroom in her thick, thigh-high bathrobe.

"I truly hoped you would be the first suitor to love me. I said the same of these before they betrayed me. Look about you. For here are my suitors, every one."

By freakish coincidence, each of the help staff stood before the exquisitely painted portrait that most bore his resemblance along the winding stair.

Gone was their period clothing of luxury they wore while in Elise's good grace, and in their place, whichever uniform and tool ascribed to their particular vocation: the masseuse with a handful of slender needles, the tailor tautly gripping his measuring tape in both hands, the chauffeur wielding a tire iron, the butler with a steaming iron, the kitchen cook clutching a cleaver, the stable marshal with shovel over shoulder, the farmer with his pitchfork, the gardener snipping his sharp shears, and the ship's surgeon-barber running his thumb along the blade of his straight razor.

The color of their flesh, now faded to gray, looked like old photographs left exposed to the elements and time.

The only unaccompanied painting was Reggie's, who presently held Howie firmly in his icy grip.

"Each loved me for a time until they grew greedy, bored, or bitter, just as you did. And just as they are, so will you be—a suitor, suited to be no more than a servant looking after my affairs, which seems to be the only part of my estate I know I can trust you with completely, Howie."

He was surprised. "That's the first time you've ever called me Howie."

"Because, my little man, Howie is a *boy's* name, and boys are made for *little* things. But don't worry your *little* mind over such matters. Leave those to bigger men than you."

"But—"

"Reggie, take him to Nicholas," she addressed his captor.

"Nicholas? You two *are* lovers," accused Howie.

"Only in the manner a servant loves her master, but you will know all about that soon enough."

Chapter Seventeen

Elise stood resplendent in her regal bridal gown. She threw the bouquet to a gaggle of giggling maidens, each eager to catch the lucky floral omen.

She and her lover ran up the red brick driveway, crushing orange blossom petals underfoot. Taking her hand in his, the groom and she ran up the familiar stone steps to the front door.

"I don't know what it is about weddings, but it almost seems rude for the bride and groom to run off to consummate the marriage," said the groom.

"O, Bartholomew, that kind of thinking is for little men."

"I really wish you would just call me Bart."

"That is a boy's name."

"Alright, alright. But still, don't you think it's just a little rude to leave all this mess for friends and family to clean up?"

"Nonsense, dear. We have servants for such menial tasks."

"Servants? Really?"

The door opened, and behind it stood the ghastly Reggie in his usual fine attire.

"Speaking of, this is Reggie, my, or should I say, our, doorman. Reggie, meet Bartholomew; Bartholomew, Reggie."

Reggie extended his hand.

When Bart took hold of the cold slab of meat, a shiver ran down his spine. "Pleased to meet you, Reggie," he said, swallowing hard. His arm convulsed in involuntary reflex to pull his hand free but he hated to seem rude.

Reggie didn't speak, but after a few perfunctory jerks that barely passed as a handshake, the limp hand fell to his side.

"So, he's the doorman," said Bart, nervously. "Who's the lucky guy who gets to clean up after everybody?" He turned to survey the grounds spread out before him.

"Oh, that would be the grounds keeper. Down there, by the new patio," said Elise.

Bart turned his attention to where Elise indicated. A stooped figure was busy placing the last bricks on the border of the nearly complete patio. He picked up another brick, then scooped a trowel into a bucket of mortar and spread a white dollop on the bottom and side of it.

"Howie," she called from the front door. "Would you be a dear and start tidying things up?"

The servant turned his head at the voice of his mistress. He saw her standing on the familiar porch in her flowing gown, her ageless beauty filling his hollow eyes with an insatiable longing to satisfy her in whatever manner she desired, for that was his sole desire.

"I hope you don't mind me saying this," started Bart, "but that guy looks like he wants to tear your clothes off, or your throat out. I'm not sure which."

"Who? Howie? He's harmless," she assured him.

"If you say so. Wouldn't want you two to be having a fling behind my back," he said, giving her a playful wink.

"Nonsense, darling. You're the first suitor who has ever loved me for who I am, and not for what I have."

He smiled at his bride, then taking her arm in his, they crossed the threshold into Sallow Manor.

GRAVE MARKER

Neil Davies

VAMPIRE
WORMS

Chapter One

They floated in on the breeze, light as gossamer, translucent in the sun hanging low and hazy over the Cheshire fields. No one noticed them. Rippling, almost invisible, they snaked over the clock tower, the church spire, the homes, and the workplaces of Taupmere, and no one knew they had arrived.

Until people began to die.

Chapter Two

Paul Walker made his tea and toast as quietly as he could, wincing at the bubbling of the kettle and the inordinately loud popping of the toaster. He didn't want to wake his sister. If he did, she would undoubtedly want him to make her breakfast, and he really didn't have the time or inclination.

He buttered the toast and ate it standing at the marble-effect kitchen unit. A round table and two chairs sat no more than three feet behind him, but he preferred to eat and drink on his feet. Dirty dishes were stacked unevenly in the sink and on the draining board. He had considered putting on the dishwasher, but the noise would wake Janet, and he had already decided he didn't want to do that.

The house was old and small, built of brick and local stone. A cottage, if you discarded the romantic, flower-framed image of the fairy tales, sitting mid-terrace in a residential suburb of Taupmere. It was barely big enough for the two of them, and yet it had once been home to both them and their parents. Now, only Paul and his sister remained.

He drank half of his tea and then, glancing at the clock, poured the rest away down the side of the dishes in the sink. It had gone on 6:00 a.m., and he needed to get moving. But before he left, he loaded the coffee machine and set it going. Janet would need her coffee when she finally woke.

Silvery slug trails disrupted the regular pattern of the hall carpet, and he sighed. Overnight, the slugs had left swirling, crisscrossing patterns that, were they anything but slime, might have been appealing. Instead, they just reminded him he needed to vacuum when he got home that evening. He could ask Janet, but it didn't seem worth the waste of breath.

Grabbing his jacket from the coat hooks under the stairs, he eased open the front door and slipped out. It was, on the whole, a good start to the day.

* * *

Janet Walker woke as the front door closed. Was it that time already?

Had she woken before Paul left, she would have asked him to make breakfast of some sort. If she thought she could keep it down. Eating was a challenge the *morning after*. Cooking was out of the question.

She shuffled out of her bedroom and down the hall to the kitchen, unknowingly breaking the pattern of slug slime with her bare feet. Her nose twitched at the smell of coffee. Paul was thoughtful like that. Knew she would need coffee when she finally faced the daylight.

Each small movement of her head pulsed pain behind her eyes, and she felt ready to allow last night's pizza to see the world again. Why did she drink so much? Why did she end up eating pizza? She didn't even like pizza! Then she remembered. It was all they had in the fridge, and she needed to eat something, anything, after her night with the bottle.

Coffee was the only thing she could face. A mug of coffee, and then some fresh air, might just blow the alcohol-dipped cobwebs away.

Chapter Three

They floated in over the buildings, silent and unseen. At first glance, it might have seemed they flew randomly, but there was a pattern, a twisting, sweeping, searching pattern.

Local businessman Ed Malone was one of the first to notice them. As he unlocked the door to Taupmere Wholesalers, he looked up and saw the one dropping out of the sky towards him.

Chapter Four

Paul picked up his unofficial work colleague two corners away from home.

Chris Benson didn't work for the company, but he was Paul's oldest friend and currently unemployed. Some days he helped Paul out for a little cash on the side.

"Did you get out without waking the old spinster?" Chris smiled as he climbed up into the van's passenger seat.

"I don't think thirty-four really classifies as old," said Paul, pulling back out onto the deserted street.

"Older than us," said Chris. "Same thing."

"Yes, I got out without waking her."

"I'm proud of you."

Chris noticed a well-thumbed paperback on the dashboard and, reaching forward, picked it up. "*Dracula*," he said. "Really? Again?"

"It's a classic," said Paul, snapping. "I like to re-read classics."

"I'm just messing with you," said Chris, shaking his head at the obvious annoyance in his friend's voice. "You sound tired. You know, you can't keep on looking after the house and your sister on your own. It'll kill you."

"When our parents died, I took on the responsibility," said Paul. "Nothing's changed."

"Janet's the oldest—"

"She's not capable!" interrupted Paul, snapping again.

Chris paused, giving Paul time to cool down. He was concerned, and this was not the first time this particular discussion had caused some tension between them. But he hoped Paul would see sense eventually. "I like Janet," he said. "And I know she has problems. But she needs to do her fair share."

"Are you going to help me with today's list?" said Paul. "Or should I just let you out here?"

Chris sighed. As always, Paul did not want to be drawn into a serious discussion about his sister. She was draining every last drop of energy from him, and yet he wouldn't talk about it. It was frustrating, but Chris knew his friend well enough to know when to back off. "When's the first pickup?" he said, putting *Dracula* back on the dashboard and glancing at the inlaid clock. 6:33 a.m.

"First pickup, 7:00 a.m.," said Paul. "We'll be early."

"Time for a break then." Chris hunkered down in the seat and closed his eyes. "Wake me when you need me. These early starts tire me out."

* * *

Paul pulled the delivery van to the curb and let the engine idle. He double-checked his paperwork. *Pickup at 7:00 a.m., Taupmere Wholesalers.*

Killing the engine, he unclicked his seatbelt and grabbed *Dracula* from the dashboard. As long as he made his pickups and deliveries on time, he could take a few minutes to catch up on his reading. The downside of the job was the pay. But money wasn't the driving force behind Paul Walker. Job satisfaction and the avoidance of too much stress were much higher priorities.

Janet did not agree. "We need more money. Why can't you get a better job? A higher paying job! You're not stupid; you're just lazy!"

He had heard the words time and again, to the point where they barely registered as they were growled at him. He *knew* they needed more money, but he didn't see why he should be the one to change his job. Janet claimed to be an artist, a painter, but she hadn't sold anything in years. She was eight years older than him, but he felt the more mature of the two.

Pushing his bitterness to the background, determined it would not spoil the start of his day, he opened *Dracula* at the scrap of paper that acted as a bookmark. He loved the Gothic, the vampire, in fiction. His collection, overflowing the small bookcase in his bedroom, ranged from the classics of Sheridan Le Fanu and Bram Stoker to more recent interpretations, like Anne Rice and Brian Lumley. He loved them all. Except for the recent trend of teenage vampires with more angst than bite.

He glanced down at his black t-shirt, black trousers, black shoes.

He caught sight of his close-cropped black hair in the rearview mirror and raised thick eyebrows in amusement. If only he had the cape and teeth to match.

Glancing momentarily towards Chris, who had begun to gently snore, he settled himself in the warmth of the morning sun coming through the windscreen and began to read. Time for a few pages. Time to immerse himself.

He jumped as something hit the car with a loud *thump*, leaving a greasy smear as it slid off the windscreen. It happened too fast for him to catch anything but the briefest glimpse, but he had the impression of something long and near transparent.

"Did you see that?" he said, turning to Chris. But Chris continued to snore, undisturbed by the noise.

Paul leaned forward, but he could see no sign of whatever had hit the windscreen. For a moment, he considered climbing out of the van and looking around, but his curiosity was not that strong, and he didn't want to waste good reading time. Instead, he pumped the washers, flicked the wipers, and managed to clear most of the smear from the glass.

Satisfying himself that it probably fell from a nearby tree, some strange piece of foliage, like sticky weed or something, he returned to Transylvania and Jonathan Harker.

Chapter Five

Sergeant Alexander Roland was a soldier and a scientist. He had been tracking the sucovermis for more than two weeks, getting closer, but never quite close enough. He knew they were up ahead, and he knew what they were capable of. He was afraid.

His Land Rover stood at a crossroads, quietly ticking over while he considered his next move. All three of the roads facing him were narrow country roads bordered by fields. An old farmhouse, looking eerily empty. A small copse of trees. A barn. There was little else to help him decide which way to drive.

He could feel a breeze blowing, but he knew that air movement, while used by the sucovermis, did not constrain them. He could not rely on it.

The old, rusted signpost named four places he knew little about: Beeston, where he had just come from, Hand Green, Taupmere, and Bunbury.

He smiled. He knew.

They were hungry. They would not travel further than necessary before feeding. And a quick check of the maps on his phone would show him the nearest supply of plentiful food.

Chapter Six

As he drew up outside the wholesalers at 6:55 a.m., Paul saw his first dead body.

The man lay half in and half out of the open doorway. Face down. Smears of blood stained the pavement by his head and around his hands and wrists.

Paul did not move from his van. He stared, sweat forming on his brow. What should he do? He quickly looked around the street but saw no one. He nudged Chris awake.

"Wha... what is it?" said Chris, mumbling as he pulled out of his nap. "You didn't have to elbow me. Just tell me to wake up."

Paul said nothing, merely pointed out the windscreen.

Puzzled and barely awake, Chris followed the direction of the finger, momentarily confused by what he was looking at. The grisly reality shocked him awake. "Shit! Is he dead?"

"I don't know!" hissed Paul. "I've not been out there to check."

"Well... you should."

"Why don't you?"

"You're the guy with the job. I'm just helping out."

They fell silent, both staring at the body through the windscreen. It was Paul who finally sighed heavily and took the responsibility.

"Call an ambulance," he said. "Or the police. Someone."

"I don't have a phone," said Chris. "You know that."

"Use mine."

"Where is it?"

Moving slowly, licking lips that had become suddenly dry, Paul reached for the mobile phone in his jacket pocket, where he always kept it.

It wasn't there.

Frantically, he searched the cab. The floor, the dashboard, the door pockets. Then, with an angry growl, he remembered.

"It's at home, charging," he said. "I didn't think I'd miss it for one day." He swallowed in a dry throat. He would have to get out of the van. He would have to go and look. It was obvious Chris wasn't about to do it.

"Perhaps he isn't dead?" said Chris, with more hope than conviction. "Perhaps he's just unconscious and needs a bit of help."

"There'll be a phone in the building," said Paul, grasping at the unrealistic hope. "I can call from there."

Chris nodded.

With his heart thumping heavily, Paul pushed open the door and climbed out. His legs shook as he began the slow walk across the street, his feet dragging with reluctance. Sweat trickled down his back, pooling at the base of his spine. When he reached the curb, he turned his eyes away from the body, focusing instead on the pavement it lay on, and those strange streaks of blood. They reminded him of something. "Slug trails," he murmured to himself, before stepping onto the curb and raising his voice. "Hello? Sir? Are you alright?" It was a stupid question, but he had to say something. Just in case.

He got no reply, no sign of even the slightest twitch or spasm.

Moving around the side of the body, keeping his distance, and carefully stepping around those strangely familiar bloody trails, he saw the exposed throat. It was pockmarked with small wounds, streaked with blood. It took a conscious effort to raise his eyes towards the face, and more to see past the holes ripped in the flesh, the wet, shining, exposed muscle.

He gasped. "Mister Malone!"

He really should have guessed. Who else would be at the wholesalers at this time of day? And if it *hadn't* been Mr. Malone, then Mr. Malone would have been standing there, wanting to know what a dead body was doing half in and half out of his place of business.

Paul spun on his heel and vomited on the pavement.

Chapter Seven

"Vampires do not exist, Mister Walker."

"Dracula was based on a real historical person."

"Did he bite people's necks and drink their blood?"

"Well… no, but…"

"Vampires don't exist!"

Paul wiped sweat-slicked palms over his face. He looked despairingly at the gaunt detective across the table. For over an hour he had sat in the grey interview room. Just him, a table, two chairs, and the detective. Answering the same questions about how he found Mr. Malone's body. He began to wonder if they suspected *he* was the killer!

"But you saw the wounds," he said, struggling to keep his voice under control, to not display the frustration and anger he felt. "And why was there hardly any blood around?"

Detective Inspector Saul Green sighed. He was not averse to watching the odd horror film himself, but this was beyond a joke.

"Mister Walker," he said, sounding tired, weary. "How many holes does your typical vampire make in a victim's neck?"

Paul frowned, puzzled at the question. "Two. But what—?"

"Mister Malone had at least a hundred. Now, I don't know what made those holes, but it wasn't someone biting him."

"But he was so white, like the blood had been drained out of him," insisted Paul, stubborn and determined.

"Blood will settle to the lowest possible level after death, Mister Walker."

"Surely that only happens after some time? Mister Malone hadn't been dead that long!"

D.I. Green sighed. He was, in general terms, a patient man. Known for it among his fellow detectives. But even he had his breaking point, and he was rapidly approaching it. "Neither you nor I are pathologists, Mister Walker," he said, failing to keep the frustration out of his voice. "I suggest we leave that kind of thing to them."

In the silence that followed, he shuffled the papers in front of him into some semblance of order. Finally, he said, "I don't think we need continue this interview any further, Mister Walker. We may need to call you back in later, but for now, thank you for your help."

"But—"

Green spoke for the recording equipment in the room, ignoring Paul. "Interview terminated, eight thirty-five a.m." He forced a smile. "Good day, Mister Walker. Thank you again for your time. We'll take it from here."

* * *

The police station sat on the back edge of town, facing the town centre, and took pride of place between a bank and a local bakery. Separating the buildings at ground level were narrow pathways leading to the carefully cultivated fields that surrounded Taupmere on all sides. Up a short but steep rise, the tangled wildness of Taup Wood dominated the skyline.

Chris stood just outside the police station, waiting. His questioning by a detective had been short and to the point. He had seen nothing, as he had stayed in the van. Paul, on the other hand, had been in there for some time, and Chris was relieved when he saw his friend finally approaching the reinforced glass doors. "What did they say?" He fell into step as Paul exited the police station.

"They don't believe me." Paul almost shook with frustration and anger. And shock.

"Did you really think they would?" Chris lowered his voice as they reached the main pavement. There were people going about their daily business, and he had no wish to be overheard.

"I saw the holes in Mister Malone's neck," said Paul. "The mess of broken skin and mangled muscle. It might not be the traditional signature of a vampire attack, but what else could it be?"

Chris had no answer and chose instead to direct the conversation to the more mundane and practical. "Did you phone Head Office?"

Paul nodded. "From the public phone in the police station's reception. Told them I was taking the rest of the day off, considering what I've been through. They didn't seem to have a problem with it."

"Good," said Chris. "So, what's the plan?"

"I'm going home after I stop at a shop and pick up some extra garlic."

Chris smiled, started to laugh, and then saw that Paul was serious. "You really believe there's a vampire in town?"

Paul shrugged. He didn't want to talk about it anymore, knowing that no one, not even his closest friend, truly believed him.

He stood for a moment longer, weighing up his options. The van remained outside the wholesalers on the edge of town. While the police were insistent on bringing him into the station in one of their vehicles, they were not so accommodating when it came to getting him back to his own. "Bus, taxi, or walk," he said finally, turning to look at Chris.

"You got any money?"

Paul shook his head.

"No? Me neither," said Chris with a smile. "Walking it is then."

Chapter Eight

After feeding, the sucovermis were too full of their victims' blood to easily lift themselves onto the air currents. Fully sated, they crawled and slid to places of seclusion, curling into protective spirals to rest. It took time for the blood to be fully digested and absorbed into their systems. But soon they would fly once again, immediately hungry and searching for more prey.

Chapter Nine

Janet found the scarf soon after she began her walk through the town.

The stores were beginning to open, so there were few people about. It would be another hour before most shoppers would stray from their homes. Another hour before it became more crowded than she found comfortable.

The scarf lay discarded, pooled on the ground behind a trashcan at the end of an alley. She had not noticed it at first, hidden in the dark shadows thrown by the wall. It was a deep red and looked to be made of a fine, shimmering material. She was immediately drawn to it. She could easily imagine something so rich and expensive flapping about her long, thin neck, looking elegant. It fit her self-image perfectly.

Would she be seen? The shopkeepers opening their doors showed no interest in her. Neither did the scattered shoppers, their heads down in personal contemplation or captivated by window displays. For a moment, she wondered who had lost the scarf and whether they would come looking for it. But then, any feelings of guilt were thrown roughly aside by desire.

She bent quickly and picked it up. And almost dropped it again instantly.

It felt *strange*. Oily. Greasy. Almost silk-like, but somehow a little too slippery. And when she first touched it, she felt it move in her hands. But she knew that was her imagination. It was just the fabric slipping between her fingers.

She suffered a brief moment of doubt, but looking good was more important than any question of comfort. She draped it around her neck and over her shoulders, suppressing a shudder that threatened to ripple through her whole body. With a grand flick of her new scarf, Janet turned on her heel and headed for home

.

Chapter Ten

Alex Roland pulled to a stop at the sign.

Welcome to Taupmere

He reached down to the floor of the Land Rover, picked up a medical neck brace, and then wrapped and fastened it around his neck. The hard plastic dug into the underside of his chin and was uncomfortable and restricting, but he felt safer with it on. As strong as they were, he didn't think the sucovermis would be able to penetrate this strengthened plastic shield. He checked the thick wristbands, the gloves, the long socks, and the heavy boots. Finally, he pulled on a General Service Respirator and tugged the hood of his jacket forward. As well covered as he was, he still did not feel completely safe.

He thought he saw one, ephemeral, fleeting, twisting in the air, but he couldn't be sure. They could be so difficult to see at times. He felt certain they were close, if not in the sky, then already feeding on the inhabitants of this small town.

Grimly, he shifted the Land Rover into gear and headed up the road towards the first buildings on the outskirts of Taupmere.

Chapter Eleven

Activity in the police station had grown hectic in the last hour. So far, sixteen deaths had been reported with the same, or highly similar, gruesome injuries as those on the body of Edward Malone.

D.I. Green sat at his desk, taking a well-earned coffee break. The phones were still ringing, the harsh tones vibrating in his head like jackhammers. But for a short while, they were not his responsibility. "I don't know how it's being done," he said to his partner, Detective Sergeant Farmer, who sat opposite him. "But it's the same person, or people, behind all of this. Has to be. And he isn't any kind of vampire."

"Vampire?" Larry Farmer, tie crooked, top shirt button undone, swirled his pen in his cup, chasing the tea-bag, watching the colour of the liquid darken. "What's this about a vampire?"

D.I. Green sighed. "The guy who found Malone's body reckons a vampire did it."

"Dracula stalking the streets of Taupmere," laughed Farmer, a peculiarly flat, humourless laugh. "Sorry I missed the interview now."

"Don't be."

"Do you think the idiot with a vampire fetish did it? Could he be behind all the others, too?"

"Not sure," said Green, sipping his drink and wishing he brought his own in as Farmer did rather than relying on the station drinks machine. "I didn't get that kind of *feeling* about him. I agree he's an idiot, but not a killer. I'm not ready to cross him off our suspect list yet, but I'm not convinced."

"Is that our suspect list of one?"

"Absolutely." He stared for a moment at the almost untouched plastic cup standing on ring-stained papers he should be working through. He pushed back his chair and stood up. "Coffee break's over. Someone's out there killing my people. I want him."

"Count me in," said Farmer, leaving his pen in the cup, the edge of the tea bag just breaking the surface of the steeping tea. "I didn't want to answer more phones anyway."

The Taupmere police force was small, with Green and Farmer the only detectives permanently stationed there, but it was fully mobilising, calling in all off-duty officers and requesting armed units from the Chester force. No one was getting away with mass murder in their town!

Chapter Twelve

"Is that you, Paul?"

Paul tried to hide the automatic sigh at hearing his sister's high, piercing voice calling from her bedroom. Chris's quiet laugh as he carried a grocery bag to the kitchen table told of his lack of success.

"Yes, it's me," said Paul. "Chris, too."

Janet appeared from her bedroom, dressed, as usual, in a long, flowing gown, with full makeup and a cigarette dangling from long, elegant, nicotine-stained fingers. "Do you like my new scarf?"

Paul glanced up at his sister. "Pink? I would have thought pink was a bit tame for you."

Janet frowned, looking down at the scarf and trying to ignore the way its texture induced sporadic clenching of her stomach. "I could have sworn it was more red when I picked it up."

Paul was uninterested in the aesthetics, but it looked expensive, and that was a concern. "Where did you find the money?" he said while Chris unpacked the grocery bag with his head down, familiar with his friend's family arguments and not wanting to be in the middle of the one he sensed was unfolding.

Janet pouted, as she had done since they were all children, playing together in the backyard, when things were not going as she wanted them. "Well," she said, a little hesitantly. "I didn't exactly *buy* it."

"You stole it?"

"I *found* it!"

Paul turned away angrily while Chris discovered an even greater interest in the shopping bag than before. "We may not have much money, Janet," said Paul, shaking his head as disappointment replaced anger. "But we don't need to go searching through other people's rubbish."

"It was on the ground, in an alley. Someone had dropped it, not thrown it away." Janet's voice had stiffened, indignation at her brother's reaction overwhelming all other emotions. "It looked too good to just leave there." She spun on her heel, putting every ounce of drama into the turn she could muster.

Paul shook his head while Chris finally felt able to disengage from the shopping bag.

As she returned to the sanctity of her bedroom, Janet mumbled to herself, "I was so sure it was red."

Chapter Thirteen

The first to feed began to revive, slowly uncurling, colour fading to translucent. They prepared to lift themselves into the air. And as they did so, they registered that the feeding had been good, and there was more in the immediate vicinity. Much more.

Signals began to flow from the creatures. Thoughts, messages sent out across the fields, away from the town.

Back to the swarm.

Chapter Fourteen

Janet sat at her dressing table, retouching her makeup in the mirror. Before her was a full collection of jars, tubes, bottles, applicators, and brushes that she had gathered over the years. It was a wide-ranging selection of makeups, skin creams, and perfumes, but there was not one truly decent name among them. They were the cheapest she could find. She suspected that if she added together the cost of all her makeup, it wouldn't buy her one bottle of an expensive scent like Cartier or Creed Royal Mayfair. Probably not even a Jimmy Choo. How could she maintain her expensive look, her self-image of elegance and style, with discount shops or a shop's own brand?

"You need to get a better job!" she shouted, although she knew that even if Paul had heard her, he would have ignored her.

She had tried again and again to persuade him to apply for better-paying jobs. She knew he had more in him than a delivery driver. Better job, more money for them both. For *her!* Then perhaps she would be more willing to venture out and meet other people rather than running home as soon as the streets got busy. Why couldn't he understand how important this was to her? So many of her problems could be solved if he was earning more money. She might even begin to paint again.

She glanced towards the scarf where she had discarded it, over the back of a chair. It was a perfect example. She shouldn't have to go picking up things in alleys just to get a decent scarf. And in the end, it wasn't even that decent. Probably a foreign rip-off. No wonder someone decided to *lose* it. "Cheap dyes fade so fast. Disgraceful."

The scarf barely had any colour at all now. Indeed, she almost felt she could see the chair through it. So pale. Hard to believe it had been such a deep red when she found it.

Turning back to the mirror, she carefully applied mascara that clumped and ran. How could she possibly manage like this?

The scarf moved.

She saw it in the reflection. A small movement. Perhaps more of a slip than a movement? It had to be a slip. But her window was closed. The air in the bedroom was still.

Fascinated, she watched, expecting the scarf to slide off the back of the chair at any moment.

Instead, it *writhed*.

She let out a small cry of surprise.

The now-translucent sucovermis tensed, gathered its strength, and attacked.

The moment before it wrapped itself around Janet's neck and lower face, a row of needle-like teeth sprang from within its twisting form.

They punctured her skin, some stabbing into her muscles, injecting her with a paralysing venom, others opening her arteries and veins. And along its whole length, it pulsated and rippled, massaging and masticating the flesh around the wounds.

Janet was able to scream once before the venom took everything but thought and pain and fear away from her.

* * *

Paul and Chris turned from pressing garlic cloves when they heard the short scream.

"What's she done now?" said Paul, finding it hard to keep the irritation out of his voice.

"Probably smudged her lipstick," said Chris.

Paul laughed, knowing that, on past experience, it would most likely be something that trivial. But he couldn't ignore it. "I'm coming," he called. "Hang on."

He pushed open the door to her room, already preparing the comments he would make. She would panic at the slightest change in her appearance. He sometimes dreaded the thought of still living with her when the wrinkles *really* began to show.

Any words died before they were spoken when he saw his sister sprawled across her dressing table, her limbs jerking spasmodically as though dancing to some unheard, arrhythmic music. And something pulsed around her neck.

Her scarf.

It was no longer pale pink, but a deep blood red. And it not only pulsed, it writhed, it shivered, it rippled around her throat.

It *drank*!

He *knew*, although it was nothing like the creatures in his books and DVDs. He *knew* it was a vampire. It was sucking the blood from his sister just as it had sucked the blood from Mr. Malone. Its colour was his sister's blood, filling its otherwise colourless body.

He thought of Mr. Malone. He thought of something hitting his van windshield, leaving a greasy smear as it slid off.

He shuddered.

Shouting for Chris's help, he ran to his sister, trying not to focus on her wide, empty, *lifeless* stare. He fought down revulsion and fear and grabbed at the creature, his fingers slipping off the gelatinous body. He held a vague hope that the garlic on his hands might help, but it seemed as ineffective as his own grasp.

Chris hurried from the other room at his shout and now joined him in his desperate attempts to dislodge the creature. They tore at the thing, clawed at it, but it did not even react to their presence.

Janet no longer moved, her limbs hanging limply, her face grey.

Crying out in rage, in frustration, Paul pounded on the creature with his fists. The body, solid with blood, barely gave beneath his knuckles.

"I need a knife," he said, almost growling the words as he turned and ran back towards the kitchen.

* * *

Chris hovered uncertainly between the still, twisted form of Janet and the bedroom door. He had not asked questions when Paul called him, but simply moved to help a friend in need. Now the questions crowded in on him. What was going on? How could Janet's scarf suddenly come alive and apparently attack her? Was he in any danger just being near the thing? With Paul out of the room, what should he do? Stay watching the creature or go and help his friend find a knife?

The initial rush of adrenaline was still in his system, but it added to his confusion rather than reducing it. Whatever he thought to do would seem, in some way, wrong.

Kitchen drawers were banging, cutlery jangling. Chris stared hopefully at the bedroom door. He no longer wanted to be alone with that thing and the ghostly white figure of Janet.

When Paul finally rushed back into the room waving a large butcher's knife, Chris almost smiled with the relief he felt. He was no longer alone.

Paul was a long way from smiling as he drew to a halt, almost stumbling as he did so. "Where is it?" he said, turning to look at Chris. "Where did it go?"

At first, Chris did not understand what Paul was saying. Where did *what* go? And how would *he* know? He turned and looked towards the dressing table, and everything became clear with an emotional crash that almost caused him to faint.

The creature had gone. It was no longer wrapped around Janet's throat. *Now* he understood what he should have been doing while Paul went for the knife. He should have been watching the creature. He got it wrong, as he knew he would.

Paul stumbled towards Janet's unmoving body. Her neck and lower face were little more than raw, bloody, chopped meat. It was obviously too late for him to do anything to help her. His redemption did not lie there. But what of the creature?

* * *

Paul resisted the crushing grief that threatened to engulf him, substituting it with anger towards the creature responsible. If it were still anywhere within his sister's bedroom, he would find it and destroy it.

Despite his desire for vengeance, he and Chris began their search cautiously. The thing had seemed fully sated, but he had no idea what that meant in terms of their search. Would it be hiding, full of his sister's blood and flesh, barely able to move, or was it, even now, preparing to attack one—or both—of them?

Chris, leaning closer to Janet than Paul could have done at that moment, was examining the floor around the dressing table. Cautiously optimistic, Paul broke off from his own search and watched his friend intently, all the while refusing to look directly at his sister's body.

"There's something here," said Chris, straightening up. "On the carpet."

Paul stepped forward, careful to keep some distance between himself and the body in the chair, but never allowing it within his line of sight. A broken trail of blood spotted the faded pattern of the thin carpet. "Slug trails," said Paul, the knife still held ready in his fist. "Just like

Mister Malone."

The trail led to a window, broken from the inside. The creature had escaped.

With immediate retribution unavailable, Paul felt the clawing emptiness of grief threatening once again. But he would not accept it. The creature may have escaped the room, but it was out there somewhere. And perhaps it was not alone? Perhaps there were others? If so, then they must all die for what the one did to his sister.

He was crying, unaware of when he had started. Angrily, he wiped the tears from his face with the back of his hand. He had no time for tears. There were vampires to track and kill!

"We have to tell the police," said Chris, breaking the melodramatic spell that had overtaken Paul. "They'll have to believe you now."

Paul said nothing, but he nodded slowly. What Chris was saying made sense, even though it lacked the visceral satisfaction of his own idea. It was in his nature to follow the rules, to do the right thing. Hopefully, the end result would be the same: the destruction of the vampires.

Chapter Fifteen

Detectives Green and Farmer climbed wearily out of their unmarked police car. Too many grieving families. Too many blood-soaked, mangled corpses sent to the morgue in Chester. Always the same method, and always no obvious trace of the killer. Scene of Crime officers were at the locations, some of them called in from surrounding towns and even Chester itself. Detective Green tried to hold some hope in that.

"Perhaps SOC will find something," he said, as they followed the footpath out of the station car park and towards the entrance.

"Perhaps," said Farmer, but without conviction. "You know, I hate to say it, but I think the bastard responsible may just be too clever for us."

"They always make a mistake," said Green, refusing to give in to his partner's pessimism, particularly as the same thought tickled at the back of his own mind. "Eventually they make a mistake."

Two police cars pulling to a stop on the double yellow lines outside the entrance interrupted them. D.I. Green read the markings on the nearest door and sighed. "Armed Response from Chester," he said. "Not sure what good they are when we don't even have a suspect."

"I thought we had a list of one?" said Farmer.

"Not much of a one at that."

Farmer nodded, watching as four dark blue uniformed officers stepped out of each Armed Response Vehicle. They all wore ballistic vests and holstered sidearms.

"Heckler & Koch USPs," said Farmer, unable to keep the obvious admiration out of his voice. "Nice handgun."

Green stopped and turned to his partner, his initial surprise fading.

"Of course. You applied to be a Firearms Officer some time ago, didn't you?"

"I did," said Farmer. "Got the chance to try out a few weapons, but then decided it wasn't for me. I'm fine shooting a gun, just don't like the idea of someone shooting back."

"And I'm sure your experience has stood you in good stead during your time here on the frontline in Taupmere."

Farmer's smile broadened into a grin. "First time I've almost felt like laughing all day," he said.

"The power of sarcasm," said Green. "I'd smile, but I'm too worn out."

"Larry?" One of the firearms officers had separated from the group and approached the two local detectives. "Larry Farmer?"

Farmer, after a moment's uncertainty, smiled with recognition. "Simon Barker," he said. "Good to see you again. I see you're a sergeant now."

"Keeping pace with you," said Barker. "Which was never that easy."

The two men shook hands vigorously while Green stayed back, not wanting to intrude on the reunion. Nevertheless, Sergeant Barker turned a friendly but curious eye in his direction. It did not go unnoticed by D.S. Farmer.

"This is my D.I.," said Farmer.

"Nice to meet you, Sir," said Barker. "I don't envy you trying to keep Larry in line."

"I do my best," said Green.

Barker glanced back towards his team, patiently waiting for him.

"I'd better get going," he said. "We've got a meeting with your Superintendent. I'm hoping we can help."

"I hope so, too," said Green as Barker turned away to rejoin his team.

"Good man," said Farmer. "He was training for the firearms team same time as me."

"I guessed," said Green.

They stayed back as the firearms officers strode into the station.

"They certainly exude a certain confidence," said Green. "Almost smugness."

"Part of the training," said Farmer. "Would you want an armed officer to look anxious and unsure? Let's give them a couple of minutes before we go in, shall we?"

"Absolutely," said Green, nodding. "Wouldn't want to be mistaken for a threat."

* * *

"Detective Green!"

Green and Farmer had given the Firearms Officers ten minutes and were about to walk into the police station when they heard the shout. They both turned. Green sighed.

"Oh shit," he murmured.

"Friend of yours?"

"Our suspect list of one," said Green.

"And his friend, the one I interviewed," said Farmer. "Maybe they want another chat?"

Paul Walker and Chris Benson were running up the road towards them. They seemed distressed, their tear-streaked faces grimacing in pain and anguish. It was a look the policemen had seen too many times that day.

"Mister Walker, what...?"

"Detective Green. My sister... It killed her... Her neck... Her face... Blood!"

Paul almost fell into the detective's arms as he stumbled, trying to slow his run. Chris shuddered to a stop behind him, gasping for air, unfamiliar with the exercise.

Green was vaguely aware that a Land Rover had rattled to a stop behind the ARVs, but his concentration was on Walker.

"*Who* killed her, Mister Walker? Did you see anyone?"

Green felt a little guilty at his first reaction on seeing the almost incoherent man standing before him. Something serious, something tragic and violent had happened. But despite the guilt, he experienced some small hope that these two young men might be the first witnesses they had. This could be the mistake by the perpetrator they'd been waiting for.

"The creature, the vampire creature… Around her neck…. Mister Malone…"

"Vampire?" Farmer sighed, catching the glance of disappointment his partner threw his way. There was no breakthrough here. It was obvious Walker had cracked under the strain of the day. Maybe finding Malone's body was just too much for him?

"He's telling the truth." Chris had finally regained his voice. "I was there. I saw it, too."

D.I. Green shook his head. The day had been hard on all of them, and he didn't need this now.

"I told you before, Mister Walker," he said quietly. "Vampires—"

"Exist!"

The interruption came from behind the detectives, and they turned to see a uniformed soldier stepping out of the Land Rover, stiff and awkward in full body armour.

Green glanced around, uncomfortably aware that people were gathering, drawn by Walker's shouting and the arrival of the soldier. The conversation needed to be moved inside as quickly and as quietly as possible.

"Look," he said to the newcomer. "I've no idea who you are,

soldier. As far as I'm aware, we haven't called in the army, and I would be grateful if you kept your wild ideas to yourself. Shall we all go inside and carry this on in a bit more privacy?"

Alex Roland glanced towards the sky. "No time, Detective. Listen. Believe me. I know what I'm talking about. I was involved in the project."

"Project?" Green wasn't sure he had heard correctly. The soldier's mask muffled his voice. "What project? You'll have to take that off. I can barely hear you."

Farmer tried to ease Walker and Benson towards the police station door while his partner talked. Why hadn't any uniforms come out to help? You could never find a policeman when you wanted one!

"The government captured a live vampire almost a decade ago, although we'd been trying much longer," said Roland, pushing the GSR up onto the top of his head. "They're not like you see on TV and in the movies. They're wild animals. Hunters, killers, without the intelligence to do anything more. A failed mutation that's refused to die." He looked towards the growing crowd of townspeople, pleased they were there. They needed to know. They needed to be warned.

D.I. Green tried to contain his growing anger. Why was everyone around him going insane? "Bullshit!" It was the only answer he could think of.

Roland continued as though there had been no interruption. His focus was on finishing his story. Making sure people knew the truth. "We extracted its DNA," he said. "This *creature* the young man saw isn't exactly a vampire, but it's a distant relation. A *manufactured* relation!

We called them sucovermis."

"And what the hell does sucovermis mean?" said Green, his voice rising in volume and pitch despite his best efforts at control.

"It's Latin, sort of," said Roland, smiling grimly. "Everything has to have a Latin name, right? We had to Google it, but we came up with one. Means bloodsucking worm." He looked at Paul, nodding. "*Vampire* worm, if you like."

Paul barely heard the words. His shifting, erratic attention had been drawn by the cloud that gathered in the sky at the far end of town. Some of the still-growing crowd had turned also, and an unsettled murmur rose about them. The cloud seemed too low, too dark, too *alive*.

Roland turned, his neck aching in the brace. He immediately pulled the GSR back down over his face. "It's too late," he said, his muffled voice almost breaking as he spoke. "The swarm has arrived!"

Chapter Sixteen

They covered the sun as they writhed and twisted their way across the town, casting an eerie, frightening darkness over the upturned faces of the people below. Too many to count, so dense in their formation that even their translucence seemed solid, the sucovermis swarm descended on Taupmere, drawn by the messages of abundant feeding sent out by the scouts.

The crowd that had been steadily growing in front of the police station panicked. People ran with no thought to direction. A scattered mass of terrified humanity, screaming their fear until their throats burned. Tripping and being tripped. Stumbling and falling as deadly ribbons wrapped around exposed skin, teeth bursting through flesh, powerful constrictions liquidising skin and muscle as the sucovermis drank.

Alex Roland, acting while others froze in shock, tugged open the door of the police station. "Get inside, quick!" he snapped, the tone of command clear even though the mask muffled his voice.

Paul and Chris obeyed immediately, hurrying into the station, ignored by the people already cowering inside the reception area. Detectives Green and Farmer hesitated. They shared a look of guilt at abandoning those fighting for their lives, people they had vowed to protect. But they also shared a need for self-preservation. And fear.

"You'll help no one by dying," said Roland, his voice breaking their hesitancy.

The two detectives hurried into the station, and Roland quickly followed them. Without a word, he crossed to the reception desk, leaned past the terrified receptionist, and activated the security lock for the doors. This was not his first time inside a police station.

"What the hell is happening?" said D.I. Green, his voice cracking with shock and fear.

"The swarm's arrived," said Roland, his muffled voice calm, unhurried. "I was too late."

"Too late for what?" said Paul and Chris simultaneously. Any other time they would have smiled.

"To save your town," said Roland. "I wanted to warn you, give you a chance—"

He was interrupted by the firearms officers bustling past him on their way to the door, their handguns already drawn.

"There's no point," said Roland. "You won't have a chance."

Sergeant Barker, leading his team, hesitated for a moment. "People are dying out there," he said. "I don't know who you are, soldier, and I don't need your opinion. We're armed police officers. It's our duty to protect those people."

"The soldier's right, Simon," said Farmer, stepping forward. "It's suicide to go out there."

"Larry," said Barker, with barely contained impatience. "It's okay for you and your D.I. to hide in here, but we're armed. With that comes a certain responsibility to step into situations unarmed officers can't."

"This doesn't have to be one of those situations," said Farmer, a note of pleading in his voice. "Please, Simon, for old time's sake. For the sake of your team. Stay inside with us."

Barker slowly shook his head. "I'm sorry, Larry. We have to do this. And we'll be fine." He smiled. "We have the weapons and the training to take on anything. You should know that." He turned towards Roland. "Unlock it, soldier."

Roland, without a word, pressed the switch behind the reception desk as Barker waved his team towards the doors.

"See you soon, Larry," said Barker. "You, too, soldier."

The firearms team, with Barker at the head, pushed their way outside.

"All very honourable and brave," said Roland, as he locked the doors once more. "But ultimately a useless waste."

* * *

For a moment, Sergeant Barker and his team hesitated, stunned by the gore-filled tableau before them. Then their training took control. If any felt confusion or surprise at the enemy they faced, none showed it.

They opened fire with their Heckler & Koch pistols while two of them ran to the rear of the ARVs, pulling LMT Defender AR-15 semi-automatic rifles from the locked boxes in the back.

The rifle fire joined the pistol fire, but hitting the twisting ribbons was a matter of luck more than skill. A small number died, translucent flesh torn from their bodies, too damaged to continue flying. Those few fell to the ground, writhing, slowly growing more still, a last twitch before they died. But there were too many, and the firearms officers were too few.

Sergeant Barker began to see the truth in what the soldier and Larry had said. He acknowledged, to himself, that he had made a potentially fatal misjudgment in rushing into the fray. Whatever these things were, they were almost impossible to hit, particularly with pistol fire.

Blake and Niven, the two officers who had control of the assault rifles, were doing slightly better. But full automatic mode had been disabled on the police rifles, and this was one situation where they could have used it.

Barker began, hurriedly, to plan for a strategic withdrawal back inside the station. He never got a chance to call the order.

* * *

Those gathered in the relative safety of the station, watched in fear and impotency as a section of the swarm detached itself and headed directly for the armed officers.

"They act like they have intelligence," said D.I. Green.

"They have," said Roland, standing nearby, still in full protective gear.

Outside, the firearms officers were ruthlessly attacked. They lost hold of their weapons and fell, screaming, as the needle-like teeth of the sucovermis punctured their flesh.

D.S. Farmer could do nothing but watch as his old colleague, Sergeant Simon Barker, fell under the onslaught, still firing his pistol as three of the creatures wrapped themselves around his exposed hands and neck.

"I'm sorry, Larry," said Green, seeing his partner's distress. "I really am."

Farmer nodded, but his eyes were on the scattered weapons of the firearms officers on the bloodied pavement. Driven by a mindless rage, and before anyone could stop him, he ran to the desk, unlocked the doors, and pushed his way out of the station.

Green tried to go after him, but Roland quickly locked the doors.

"It's too late, Detective," said the soldier. "There's no point both of you throwing your lives away."

* * *

D.S. Farmer snatched up a pistol from the pavement, its grip slick with blood. He opened fire.

Bullets found human flesh as well as that of the creatures gorging themselves. But the officers were already dead, and Farmer was determined to kill the things that had slaughtered the men. Had his career gone differently, he could have been one of those officers, lying dead alongside his old colleague, Simon Barker.

"Larry!" D.I. Green, inside the police station, shouted through the glass, hovering uncertainly between his own safety and the compulsion to help his partner. "Come back in, Larry. Leave them."

Farmer was unaware of his partner's dilemma. It was doubtful he even heard him. As one gun emptied, he dropped it and picked up another, strangely calm now that he had decided his purpose. He did not even seem to care as one of the creatures, twisting and writhing through the air, attacked from the side.

Green cried out in helplessness as his friend and partner tugged at the ribbon that snaked around his neck.

For one moment, D.S. Farmer seemed finally aware of the shocked onlookers inside the station, staring back at them with eyes that were already glazing over. Then there was a burst of intense, burning pain, and he fell, twitching in death, by the station steps.

* * *

Paul had watched the unfolding drama in horror. He turned to look at those gathered in the station, at D.I. Green, unashamedly sobbing on his knees. They were all too frightened to step outside, too frightened to even question the authority of the strange soldier as he ordered windows barred, doors barricaded.

"Are you okay?" said Chris, seeing his friend's eyes glazing. "Paul?"

Paul did not reply. His head was full of images of flying ribbons, of blood, his sister, vampires. He listened to the screams outside, and the heavy slapping of the creatures on the windows and glass doors of the station as they tried to find a way in. He heard the shouted orders and more than one person's quiet sobbing and thought that perhaps he should be crying, too. But the depth of feeling required for tears was no longer there.

"What can we do?" he said, his voice breaking

"The attack will finish when the sucovermis are sated," said Roland. "So, we wait."

"What if they break through the doors or windows?" said Chris.

"Then we die," said Roland, his voice flat, emotionless. "But until then, we wait."

Chapter Seventeen

The final scream of the dying cut sharply through the air just over twenty minutes later. The attack on the town and the siege on the police station had seemed to last much longer to the stunned, horrified people huddled together inside the reception area.

The toughened glass of the windows and doors had cracked but not shattered. Repeated attacks had shaken jagged patches of plaster from the walls, but the concrete behind had not been breached.

Paul stepped cautiously to the windows, where it was all but impossible to see through the intersecting streaks of smeared blood. All he could say with any certainty was that there were dead bodies. Twisted, ripped, mangled bodies. Had his personal fear not drained him of all empathy, he would have cried, perhaps even felt nauseated. Instead, he felt nothing, and that scared him more than anything.

He looked to Chris, to D.I. Green, to the other survivors, and saw pain, grief, sadness. He could not identify with them. He felt he had more in common with the soldier. A man such as that would understand the need for detachment, for the lack of emotional involvement.

The lack of *empathy*. He would have faced such things before, Paul had no doubt about that. To empathise with all would lead to insanity. Detachment was a necessity, not a flaw.

* * *

Silence had fallen over the survivors, as it had fallen over the town outside. A heavy, smothering silence that was more ominous, more frightening, than the cries and pleas of the dying. Silence meant death on a scale none of those present had seen before. Except one.

Alex Roland pulled off the CSR and looked at the few people he had managed to save. So few, maybe thirty or forty at the most out of the whole town. He was disappointed. He had hoped to save more.

He noted the young man sitting nearby, staring at him. The man's eyes had a glaze he recognised, one he saw when he looked in a mirror. He felt sorry for the man. "What's your name?" he said.

"Paul Walker."

"Well, Paul Walker, you should try to *feel* something. Those are the residents of your town out there, dead. You'll know some of them. Try to feel, or it can become a habit. Not feeling. A dangerous habit."

"I see it in you."

Roland sighed. "It's too late for me. I need to be this way to do what I'm trying to do. You don't. You're not me."

"What is it, exactly, that you're trying to do?" said Paul.

Roland ignored the question and raised his voice, addressing all the survivors. "You have maybe half an hour to get away from here before the sucovermis start feeding again."

"Mister Walker asked a good question," said D.I. Green, recovering some semblance of control and trying not to think of his partner, lying dead on the other side of the door. "You tried to warn us about these things. Is that it? You're trying to save people's lives?"

"I do it as much for myself as for others," said Roland, bowing his head. "I'm no hero. I'm trying to purge myself of more guilt, more culpability than you could ever imagine."

"To do with those things," said Paul.

"The sucovermis," said Roland. "Yes. I was part of the team that created the sucovermis. When they escaped, I was one of those who insisted we immediately track them down and either capture or destroy them." He sighed, feeling a little uncomfortable with all the survivors listening intently. "Those higher up the chain of command felt differently. They decided that, while the escape was an accident, it provided the perfect opportunity for a field test. The orders were to observe and report, but not to obstruct or interfere with the sucovermis in any way. Whatever the cost."

"But those things are killing people," said Chris, incredulous. "Surely your bosses wouldn't order you to just stand by and do nothing while they killed people?"

"They *designed* the sucovermis to kill people," said Paul, understanding. "Why would they stop them? It's not a true test of their destructiveness if they're interfered with. What's a few hundred, a few *thousand* innocent people's lives as long as we end up with an effective new weapon?"

"But you tried to warn us," said D.I. Green to Roland. "You tried to interfere."

"I deserted," said Roland, a slight smile twitching the corner of his mouth. "I couldn't do what they asked, so I ran. I've been tracking the scouts, ahead of the swarm. Trying to warn people to get away. Trying to assuage my guilt by saving those I can."

"What about those that *could* follow the orders?" said Paul grimly. "I presume they're following, too?"

"They're following the swarm," said Roland, nodding. "There'll be a clean-up squad on the way here. We really need to get moving."

"Clean up?" said Green. "What are they cleaning up? The creatures?"

"The dead bodies," said Roland, drawing his pistol and checking it was loaded. "And they don't like witnesses either. They won't risk leaving anyone to talk about all this."

In the silence that followed, the implications of his words were slowly absorbed by the townspeople. They, the survivors, were a potential danger to this terrible field test. They were a hitch in the ruthless plan of those in charge. They needed to be removed. Eliminated.

Paul could not decide whether the lack of panic among his fellow survivors was a testament to their courage or the deadening effect of sheer terror. Either way, he was relieved. He preferred the heavy silence to manic noise.

"Now," said Roland, breaking the silence. "I'm leaving. There's a target on my back ten times bigger than on any of yours. I can't afford to be spotted by the clean-up squad. I need to track the scouts and warn the next town. Hopefully, I'll be more successful than I was here."

"But you did save some of us," said Chris.

"We can thank you for that," said D.I. Green. "You've given us a chance."

"Then I suggest you take it," said Roland. "And get moving." He looked directly at Paul. "You, too. And try to feel *something*!"

* * *

They had to push hard on the unlocked doors to open them, sliding a ravaged body out of the way as they did so.

Bodies lay all around, a grim landscape of painful, violent death. Blood stained the roadway, running into the gutters and down the drains. The pavement, too, was slick with gore, and they trod carefully as they exited.

D.I. Green paused a moment beside the body of his partner, but he knew this was not the right time for grieving or sentimentality. With a heavy sigh, he quickly moved on, stepping to Paul's side and placing a gentle hand on the young man's shoulder. "You were right," he said. "There *are* vampires. Just not quite as you expected."

"No," said Paul. "These are much worse."

"Couldn't we just find the things while they're sleeping and kill them?" said Chris, joining D.I. Green and Paul.

"If you could find them all," said Roland, standing just ahead and turning to face them. "But you wouldn't have long, and there are hundreds of them in a swarm. You'd never manage it."

"So we run," said Chris.

"We run," agreed Paul. "If we're lucky, we might live."

"I need to go, too," said Roland. "I do *not* want to be around when the clean-up—"

His forehead burst open in a fantail of blood and bone as the sniper's bullet drilled through from the back of his skull, just missing D.I. Green and shattering a window in the police station behind.

For a moment, Roland's eyes seemed to widen in surprise, and as ridiculous as it was, Paul half expected him to speak, to just shrug off the bloody hole in his head as some minor itch. But then the legs folded, and Roland fell.

Paul considered how graceless it had been. No slow motion. No artful twisting and tumbling. No last words. Real death was not like those he watched nightly on his DVDs. It was messy and quick and untidy.

Still, he felt nothing but slight disappointment. And an awareness that he should move, quickly.

The distant rumble of trucks disturbed the eerie silence. A cloud of exhaust fumes rose at the far end of town.

"The clean-up team," said Paul, grabbing Chris's arm. "We should run!"

D.I. Green hesitated as the two young men turned and ran for the back of the police station, where the fields and, further on, the trees of Taup Wood might offer some protection. He knew he should follow, but he was still a policeman, the most senior one still alive, and he felt a responsibility towards the men and women who stood, confused and afraid, on the pavement and road in front of the station.

"We need to go," he said, having to raise his voice to be heard over the growing babble of indistinct words coming from those gathered. He could hear the beginnings of panic in the voices, and it seemed to have frozen them where they stood. "We've got to escape!" he shouted. *I should escape*, he thought. *To hell with the rest. But it goes against everything I believe, every reason I took this job.*

He was still hesitating as the military convoy rumbled up to the police station, rolling over bodies, crushing bones beneath heavy wheels. As armed soldiers disembarked from their carriers, Green glanced nervously back towards the body of Larry Farmer and the still-loaded gun inches from his lifeless fingers. *I'm dead anyway*, he thought. *Why not take a chance?*

He was trying to build the courage when an army Land Rover at the tail-end of the convoy pulled to a stop at the curb in front of him. Behind the wheel, a young soldier sat upright, staring straight ahead. A driver for someone of higher rank. Green was just trying to peer past the young man to see who was being driven when the passenger door opened.

* * *

Lt. Colonel Draper, initially deployed to babysit a group of scientists until the accidental breakout made things more interesting, looked at the dead littering the street and felt nothing. They were not people; they were simply a problem he needed to clean up. The same held true for the living.

His men had spread out, covering those residents standing, watching. This did not look like it would be difficult.

"Who are you?"

The shout came from a thin, middle-aged man, and Draper stared at him silently for several seconds before finally deciding to reply. "Lt. Colonel Draper, British Army," he said. "And who might you be?"

"Detective Inspector Green, Taupmere Police," said Green, emboldened now that his first question had been answered. "You have no jurisdiction here, and your soldiers would seem to be threatening unarmed civilians."

"And what would you have us do, Detective Inspector Green?" said Draper, smiling.

"Leave."

"Can't do that, I'm afraid," said Draper, shaking his head. "I have a job to do, just as you do. It just so happens that mine is more important."

"Says who?" said Green, swallowing back his nervousness. Maybe if he could keep this Lt. Colonel talking, they could avoid a slaughter.

"People much higher up the food chain than either of us, Detective Inspector."

Draper stepped round the Land Rover, walking towards Green, stopping when he reached the body of Alexander Roland. He contemplated the dead man in silence for some moments while D.I. Green looked on nervously. "Sergeant Roland," Draper eventually said. "Such a promising career in both science and the army. Thrown away because of stupid morals and juvenile idealism."

"He didn't want to see innocent people killed," said Green, feeling he should defend the man who had tried to help his town.

"He got his priorities screwed up," said Draper, still not looking up from the body. "He's a deserter. A traitor!"

Draper pulled the Glock 17 Gen 4 pistol from the holster at his side quickly and smoothly. Without pause, he shot the already dead Roland twice in the head. D.I. Green flinched as the body jerked and fresh blood, bone, and brains spattered the surrounding pavement.

Draper did not holster his pistol. "As you can see, Detective Inspector," he said, looking up. "I do my job well, and I do it thoroughly."

D.I. Green knew, at that moment, that there was no reasoning with this man. Whatever he said would not change the outcome. Lt. Colonel Draper fully intended to massacre every living person in Taupmere. There would be no witnesses to the horrific field test of the army's newest weapon.

The question of whether to take the risk was no longer a question. He had no choice.

He dived for the pistol by his dead partner's hand.

A burst of assault rifle fire tore screams from some of those standing nearby. The bullets thudded into D.I. Green's back, ripping through his internal organs, punching their way out through his chest and stomach. He had no time to think. He was dead before he hit the ground.

Draper had not needed to lift his own weapon. His men were as good and as thorough as he was.

Chapter Eighteen

Paul and Chris, both gasping from exertion, reached the tree line of Taup Wood and hid inside its gloom and shadows. They turned back to watch events in the town just as D.I. Green was gunned down.

"Jesus!" said Chris, flinching. "They're really going to do it, aren't they? They're really going to kill everyone."

Paul said nothing, just nodded.

In the town below, people were finally moving, trying to run in a mass panic.

The soldiers opened fire, dropping most of the people with their first burst. With robot-like efficiency, they stepped forward, ensuring no one escaped, firing until all the survivors of the sucovermis attack were on the ground. They moved among the bodies, finding any wounded and shooting them through the head.

The two young men the soldiers were, for the moment, unaware of, continued to hide in the woods, watching. Chris was crying. Paul felt somewhere that he, too, should be crying, but he didn't want to;

he could not make himself. He knew the soldier had told him to try and feel something, but he felt nothing.

Once the slaughter was over, the soldiers shouldered their weapons and began the clean-up of bodies. They worked in pairs, lifting a body between them and throwing it into the back of the last truck in the convoy. To the watching Paul, the growing pile lost focus, the edges blurring. It no longer seemed possible to discern individual people, twisted limbs, or staring, screaming heads. It was a grotesque work of abstract art, the shapes meaningless, the message lost in the slipping, shifting morass of flesh.

Pulling his gaze away from the truck, Paul noted a number of soldiers on the perimeter of the body collection area. Each one held a small tablet, their concentration on the screen. "What do you think they're looking for?" he said.

Chris, his pallor grey, the scars of dried tears streaking his face, watched the soldiers for a moment before a weary shrug of his shoulders answered the question more succinctly than words.

"They're looking for something," said Paul. "What happens when they find it?"

Almost before he finished speaking, the perimeter soldier nearest the police station raised his arm and shouted something unintelligible to Paul. But it was obvious the soldiers around him understood.

All of the soldiers, including those on the perimeter, hurried in an orderly fashion back into their convoy vehicles. Windows were closed, doors double checked.

"What are they doing?" said Chris, breaking his silence. "Are they leaving? But there are still bodies on the ground."

"Look over there, to the left," said Paul, nudging Chris in the right direction. "There's your answer."

Chris looked as the first of the reviving sucovermis rose from the industrial park on the edge of town, like the faint ripples of a heat haze, flowing upwards. They were quickly followed by others from residential streets, shop buildings, restaurants, everywhere they had hidden themselves to rest. They massed in the sky above the town and descended as one on the military convoy. Once again, hundreds of the creatures flitted and writhed outside the police station, but there was little of the ferocity they had displayed earlier as they tried to get into the vehicles. To Paul, it seemed they knew it was hopeless.

"Will they come for us?" said Chris, his voice trembling. "Can they sense us?"

"It's possible the scent of the woods will mask us," said Paul, his voice steady, untroubled. "But even if they did sense us, there's only two of us. They're looking for more food than that, and they're waiting for their scouts to tell them they've found it. I think we're safe."

As he finished speaking, the swarm, as one, retreated from the convoy. In eerie silence, they flew away from Taupmere, roughly following the east road.

"Guess the scouts have found something," said Paul.

He and Chris watched as the soldiers climbed back out of their vehicles and continued with their grisly clean-up. At that same moment, Paul noticed other military vehicles arriving, spreading out onto the side roads, deploying along the very same residential streets that the sucovermis had risen from. Others occupied the industrial park. Still others the outlying shops and businesses. He felt Chris shudder as they watched soldiers, on foot, sweeping from house to house, building to building. They could not see what happened inside, but they heard the distant crackle of gunfire.

"It's a massacre," said Chris, in tears once more. "An atrocity. We should have had your phone with us. We could have filmed it, got some proof."

"And showed it to who?" said Paul, still finding it hard to feel anything other than a mild anger and a stronger interest in events. "Face it, Chris. Phone or not, there's nothing we can do."

It took a long time to move all the bodies from the town centre and clean the blood from the streets and pavements with a jet hose. Similar actions were taking place in all areas where the military vehicles had unloaded their armed cargo. A lengthy but meticulously performed task. When the convoy finally rumbled out of town, following the direction of the swarm on the east road, the sun had almost fallen below the horizon.

"Somehow, we're alive," said Chris, laughing with relief through his slowly drying tears. "I didn't think we'd make it. But all those people dead. The whole town, for Christ's sake."

"No witnesses," said Paul. "Just like the soldier said."

"But *we* are witnesses," said Chris. "So, what do we do now? Who can we trust in any position of authority when it's the army and, presumably, the government behind it? Who do we tell this to?"

"No one would believe us," said Paul. "And anyone we talk to could be part of it."

"So, what *do* we do?"

"We walk," said Paul. "If we cut cross-country we should be able to get ahead of the scouts. Not at the next town, or even the one after that, but eventually."

"For what purpose?" said Chris. "Other than to get ourselves killed!"

"To carry on the work of the soldier," said Paul. "To try and warn other towns of what's on the way and hope they believe and run."

"Carry on the work of the soldier?" Chris was incredulous. "Why?"

"Because it's the best thing we can do. And we owe him."

Paul turned and began to work his way through Taup Wood, feeling his way in the gathering darkness.

Chris, after a moment's hesitation, followed him. He wasn't sure he totally agreed with Paul's reasoning, but Paul was his best friend, and the two of them were unique. Surviving witnesses. It didn't seem a bad idea to try and help others become survivors, too. And who knew? Perhaps, eventually, there'd be enough survivors that someone in authority would have to listen. Someone who was not already corrupted by the desperate desire for a bigger, more deadly weapon than the supposed enemy. If that person existed. It was worth a try.

The two survivors disappeared in the gloom of the sunset as the last light brushed the tops of the trees with an ethereal glow. Somewhere ahead, that same glow was falling on the floating, twisting bodies of the sucovermis scouts and the following swarm as they neared their next, unsuspecting target.

Author's Note

"Vampire Worms" started life as "Ribbons of Blood," a short story that appeared in my first collection, The Midnight Hour, back in 2007. "Vampire Worms" is an extended version of that story.

ABOUT THE AUTHORS

Joseph Rubas is the author of over 200 short stories and several novels. His fiction has appeared in *The Horror Zine; Nameless Digest; Shadowland; Thuglit; All Due Respect;* and many others. His first novel, *Dracula 1912,* was published in 2016. He currently resides in New York State.

A resident of North Carolina's Outer Banks, **A.P. Sessler** frequents an alternate universe not too different from your own, where he searches for that unique element that twists the everyday commonplace into the weird. When he's not writing fiction, he composes music, makes art, and muses about theology and mind-hacking. He also likes to dress in funny clothes and talk about the first English colony in the New World.

Neil Davies was born in 1959 and has found everything else to be an uphill struggle. He currently lives in the North West of England with his wife, two grown-up children and a cat. He divides his spare time between writing, painting and music. For more information please visit his official website — http://www.nwdavies.co.uk

Press
Presents

Grave Markers, Volume Three
(includes Dominic Stabile's *Full Moon in the West*,
Adrian Ludens's *Bottled Spirits*, and S.L. Williams's *The Dance*)

Grave Markers, Volume Two
(includes Hal Badner's *Tolerance,* Sebastian Bendix's *Shriek of the Harpy,* and Russell Coy's *The One Who Lies Next to You*)

A collection of chilling tales by three distinct voices in the horror genre!

Grave Markers, Volume One
(includes Richard Black's *Nikolis Cole: the Low-Rise Saint*, Sebastian Bendix's *Rock, Paper, Scissors*, and Joshua Rex's *Coattails*)

And be sure to check out

THE DEMON GUARDIAN

Neil Davies